Heroine

'Gail Scott has an extraordinary ability to compress scenic observations ... into short, jewel-like notations. Her work often has the appearance of mosaic, of a myriad of terse, gleaming, sharded crystalline pieces of apperception placed next to one another in almost nightmarish patterns. She has a remarkable deftness of montage, of cutting from one time sequence to another without blurring.... This delicacy of montage helps to give her narratives remarkable intensity and rapidity of pace, which excites specific responses in her readers.'

– Hugh Hood

'Nothing I've read since satisfies my desire for density and beauty. *Heroine* reaches beyond the visible, touching the scarred narrative tissue inside the head, that we have blocked and injured so long. Here memory is not "the past" but imbues vitally the moment, as desire *(wherein the future creates itself)*. As in Lorca's New York, desire is inscribed in the city; the city itself is tied with love. The obsessive desire for the man, for the women, is not the true desire, but is at the same time wound and reflective surface, narrative skin eroticized every place, bringing the woman out of her woundedness, her apraxia, her inner stubborn blows..., *The trick is to look toward the future thus cancelling out nostalgia.*'

– Erin Mouré

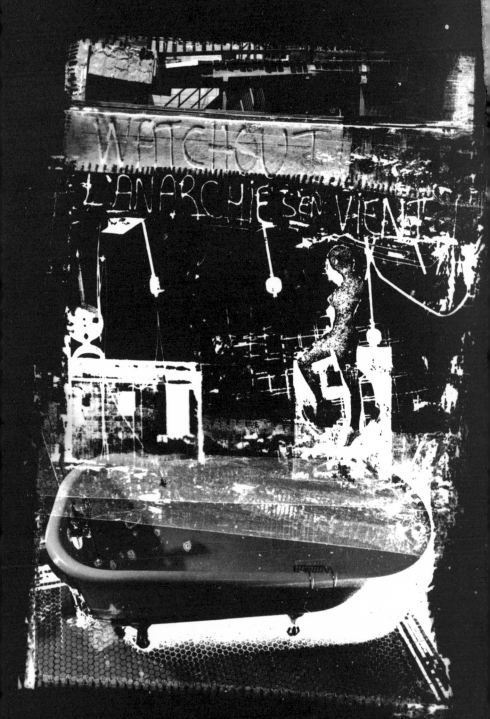

HEROINE

BY GAIL SCOTT

THE COACH HOUSE PRESS

TORONTO

Short excerpts from this novel have appeared in
Writing and *Rubicon,* as well as in the anthology
Fatal Recurrences (Véhicule Press).

Short term grants from The Ontario Arts Council,
le Ministère des Affaires culturelles and the
Canada Council helped make this project possible.

The epigraph on page 5 translated from the French
by G.S.

Published with the assistance of the Canada Council
and the Ontario Arts Council

Fourth Printing

Canadian Cataloguing in Publication Data

Scott, Gail
Heroine

ISBN 0-88910-342-9

I. Title

PS 8587.C623H47 1987   C813'.54   C87-094525-4
PR9199.2.S35H47 1987

We use signs and the signs of signs only in
cases where the things themselves are lacking.

UMBERTO ECO

I. BEGINNING

Sepia

Sir. You can on-ly put ca-na-dian monee in that machine. No sir. No foreign objects nor foreign monee in that macheen. It's an infraction you see. The guard's finger runs tight under the small print. The wooden squirrels in the rafters are si-lent. The Black tourist descends the steps with an astonished stare towards the telescope aimed at the city skyscrapers.

I'm lying with my legs up. Oh dream only a woman's mouth could do it as well as you. Your warm faucet's letting the white froth fall over the small point on the tub floor. Your single eye watches my floating smiling face in its enamel embrace.

Outside the shops swing. The wind has turned the trees to yellow teeth. This is the city. Montréal, P.Q. I work here. I'm a c....

That is I worked here til one day. I was sitting in that Cracow Café on The Main with its windows and walls sweating grey against the winter. Eating steamies made from real Polish sausage. Suddenly I looked up and there was this funny picture. A cross stuck in a bleeding loaf of bread. You were sitting under it smiling at me through your round glasses. Sort of, with your wonderful mouth, so feminine for a man's. And your beat-up leather jacket.

Some hookers were standing round drinking hot chocolate. One was so wired up she kept doing a high step still holding her cup. Right leg over left leg. Twice. Left leg over right. There was no point trying to stop her. Somehow you managed to slide out over the torn red plastic seat and sit down beside me. Without anybody seeming to mind. I loved the smell of your cracked leather jacket. From Europe with love.

No, I'm telling stories. Maybe these women were your socialist revolutionary comrades trying to get stopped for soliciting so they could expose the brutality of the city administration. Some of them had middle-class skin.

I mean solidarity. If anyone asks, instinctively I have the answer. Loving women. In my case two. That is the same set of brown eyes twice. We're side by side on her bed. Then I'm lying on top of her soft breasts. She pulls up her white night shirt and pulls down her panties so our genitals will touch. I – I think I rolled off. Yes it was me who stopped. Knowing I'm a failure. No. Never admit. Never admit you're a failure.

The smell of coffee. Real cappuccino. A few leaves rush by a real prostitute bending her knees til her pussy comes forward. Then putting her hand on it. The harsh note is in the next booth saying 'she should adopt a more self-critical voice.' His woman companion nods but her answer's drowned in the noise. 'You have a relationship,' the guy is saying, 'and you learn something from it. Next time you select better, that's all.' He shrugs. We get up to go. I like how your glasses hang on a string. When you're not wearing them. Later looking at the photos I notice we've seen it all the same. That pretty prostitute her jeans just right snugly over the V-shape but not too tight – Um, your hands reassure me. Confidently clicking the camera. Together we're crossing the bar of light.

Colder times are coming. The Black tourist sees the plain whiten beneath the skyscrapers. The scene shifts to that dome-shaped café full of hippies and women in cloche-shaped hats.

The sign says Bauhaus Brasserie. It only fills half the lens. Jane Fonda goes by on a horse spattered with the blood of Viet Nam. A gay man is fingering my homemade leather blouse and saying: 'Sweetheart you look so much like Barbarella.'

The new man and I get up to go. As we step out into the snow a woman comrade cries: 'How come you never kiss anyone but her anymore?' I'm a bit scared. We're standing in the harbour. The gulls clack in the fog over the old schooner. I can't hear my breath. Maybe we're coming in unison. The illusion of perfect fusion. 'Gail's friends are my friends,' you say in a soft voice. I'm so relieved. It's starting to snow. Of course I didn't know what you mean when you say that. Until I looked back and saw her head on your shoulder. Across the room at Ingmar's when the sun shining through the lead glass delineated that dark place under your chin where it felt so safe. I'd been running from chair to chair on those Marienbad squares asking: 'Have you seen Jon?' as if I didn't care. Suddenly she's standing in front of me saying: 'Why don't you just relax?'

She's right, Sepia. What I learned from her is that the relaxed woman gets the man. That was in the summer of 76. When the RCMP hinted our group should leave the city if we didn't want any trouble. The whole Montréal left was on the train. We called it our Olympic Vacation. Going to visit the other Founding Nation.

On that trip you're in the woods for a good two days. Deep in reserve country with the trees leaning recklessly over the horizon. My legs were so anxious I wanted to jump off. Because I couldn't forget the restaurant scene where someone said at the next table: 'Elle a perdu; qui perd, gagne.' I wrote faster. So fast and so small you could hardly see my handwriting. The cop at the counter watched as if I were writing in code. His handcuffs were at his belt. The gulls flew over the glassed-in roof. You used to sit there and think of sound, of the ships battering up and down between the waves. (I loved your mouth; it held me to you when the rest of your body cut like a knife.) You said: 'I want to be free. No monogamy. It's not for me.' I laughed and pulled out my plum lipstick. 'Tea for two,' I said. 'Decadence for me and decadence for you.' No wonder you looked surprised. It wasn't the right reaction.

Anyway we were on the train. When suddenly I was awakened by a guardian angel in a turquoise blazer. She held a CN card in her hand which said: 'While on this train your wish is my command.' We watched her disappear in the night. Noting we'd forgotten to say the heat was pouring out from underneath the seat. Though it was the middle of summer. We never saw her again.

But I couldn't get back to sleep. I was so worried about not being able to smile when the girl with the green eyes put her hand on your thigh.

> A feminist (I kept repeating)
> cannot be impaled
> by a white prince.

The trip was like a dark tunnel. At the other end there would be light. When I got to Vancouver, I'd see, maybe, how to be free. Janis Joplin came on the radio. Her voice cracked like one of those evergreens trying to grow on the burnt earth outside Sudbury. She said: *There's no tomorrow, baby* (laughing her head off). *It's all the same goddamned day. We learned that coming here on the train.*

The Dream Layer

Tis October. On the radio they're saying ten years ago this month québécois terrorists kidnapped the British Trade Commissioner. I was at my kitchen table. Through my window the mellow smell of autumn leaves in the alley. Making me slightly ill due to a temporary pregnancy. A drunk wove along the gravel. I was just wondering how to put it in a novel when the CBC announcer said: 'We interrupt this program to say the FLQ has kidnapped Britain's trade representative to Canada.' I couldn't help smiling. Even a WASP, if politicized, can recognize a colonizer. Besides the crisp autumn air always made me restless. Later, my love, we laughed so hard when the tourist agent told the group from Toronto looking for cultural manifestations in Montréal: 'Eh bien ici les *manifestations* ont lieu d'habitude au mois d'octobre.' Winking at us in line behind them (we were going to Morocco). For in French *manifestation* also means political demonstration. He meant the October Crisis and other assorted autumn riots. People were freer then.

Alors pourquoi Marie a-t-elle dit que je ne serai pas au rendez-vous? She meant on the barricades of the national struggle. Her face had this funny look, half guilty, half cruel. (She was still in the revolutionary organization then.) Even hinting that my grandfather might be Métis didn't convince her. Of course I didn't tell her and the other comrades the family kept it hidden. Why should I? They must have guessed anyway, because M, one of the leaders, tugged his beard and said: 'We're materialists. We believe one is a social product, marked by the conditions he grew up in. You're English regardless of your blood.' We were sitting in the revolutionary local. Around the table no one said a word. Even you my love, I guess you wanted to keep out of it.

Marie's face had that funny look again today when she came to visit. She was wearing an immaculate silk scarf. Over it her nose turned aside as if offended when she saw the state of my little bed-sitter. Grant it, it's kind of tacky. Green patterned linoleum and an old sofa. In the bathroom, black and white tiles like they have in the Colonial Steam Baths. Except some are falling off. Trying to make light of it, I said as we stepped into the room: 'Ha ha, the hard knocks of realism.' She didn't laugh. She didn't even smile ironically. So I decided to hold back. Refusing to explain how I'm using this place for an experiment of living in the present. Existing on the minimum the better to savour every minute. For the sake of art. Soon I'll write a novel. But first I have to figure out Janis' saying *there's no tomorrow, it's all the same goddamned day.* It reminds me of those two guys I once overheard in a Bar Salon: 'Hey,' said one, except in French. 'Did you know the mayor's dead?' His lip twitched. 'No kidding,' said the other. 'When?' 'Tomorrow, I think.' They both laughed. Sure enough the next day on the radio they said the mayor was at death's door. Nobody knew why. City Hall was mum. Rumour had it he'd crumbled with a stroke. Or else there'd been an assassination attempt by some unnamed assailant. I felt like I'd seen a ghost.

I got that same feeling again later taking a taxi along Esplanade-on-the-park. On my knee was the black book. The budding trees were whispering, the birds were singing: a beautiful spring eve. (Like when we first fell in love, my love.) When suddenly on the sidewalk I see a projection of my worst dreams. A real hologram. You and the green-eyed girl. Right away I notice she's traded in her revolutionary jeans for a long flowing skirt. And her hair is streaked. Very feminine. As for you you're walking sideways, the better to drink her in. With your eyes. Oh God, obviously you can't get enough. The taxi dropped me at the bar with the little cupid holding grapes in front of the mirror where I was going to meet some gay writers. One of them said: 'Chérie, you look terrible.' I was speechless. All I could think was what a coincidence. Because at the moment I saw you my love, I'd been writing in the black book (not believing yet that our reconciliation was really finished): *He's Mr. Sweet these days. I'm the one who's fucking up, making scenes. Oh well, tomorrow's another day.*

'Qu'as-tu?' asked Alain. He has green eyes like my father, but he wears jewellery.

I said: 'I think I've seen a ghost. A real-life scene from a nightmare I once had. Everything came back exactly as it was.'

'Trésor', dit-il, 'La science dit que la répétition n'existe pas. Les choses changent imperceptiblement de fois en fois. Maintenant tu vas prendre un bon verre.' I didn't reply, concentrating as I was on how to be a modern woman living in the present while at the same time finding out who lied, my love, me or you?

A delicious warm sweat is forming on the bathroom tiles. Through the open door I see the dented sofa where Marie sat this afternoon. Determined as ever with her flat stomach and her straight back. In that immaculate white silk. Suddenly she put her hand over her mouth, as titillated as a little girl who's caught a glimpse of something unspeakable. I knew it was that place above the stove where the dirt adheres to the grease, working the paint loose until it starts to peel off. And she was about to criticize my housecleaning. To ward it off I focused on how growing up over that dépanneur in St Henri probably made her fussy. Every Monday and Thursday after school she had to take off her blue tunic and scrub and scrub the slanting floor under the domed roof. What got her was the darkness of the courtyard. You could feel it from the kitchen window. One day, walking in there she found a big rat lounging on the table. Slowly unwinding his virile tail, he looked at the little girl with his small eyes and said: 'Mademoiselle, voulez-vous me ficher la paix?' In International French. She couldn't think of a thing to say. None of the neighbours spoke like that. Later she thought it was a dream.

Glancing only slightly in my direction, she blurted it out in spite of herself: 'Tu pourrais faire un peu de ménage. On dirait que tu n'as plus d'amour-propre.'

I kept silent. It's better than saying: 'What about you? You're too obsessed with how things look.' Besides, as I'd decided to take a bath, I was busy with my ablutions.

I guess I lost track of time. Because I didn't see her get up and say goodbye. I realized she hadn't said anything about coming back.

Colder times are coming. In the telescope the plain whitens. The Black tourist sees a field of car wrecks below the skyscrapers. A woman is walking towards a park bench. Suddenly she sits, pulling her coat down in the front and up in the back in a single gesture so you can hardly tell she's taking a pee.

Oh faucet your warm stream is linked to my smiling face. Outside the shops swing: peanuts, blintzes, persian rugs. Marie m'a dit: 'Tu as payé de ton corps.' Shhh. Reminiscences are dangerous. Who said that? Never mind. When I get out of here I'm going to throw out those old pictures on the stool by the tub. That one half-hidden in the folds of the second-hand lime green satin nightgown must have been taken in Ingmar's courtyard. Black and white with a silvery grey light shining on the shoulders of our dark leather jackets. We were the perfect revolutionary couple, tough yet happy. Leaning together after a walk in the Baltic fog eating almond-cream buns. Except at Ingmar's somebody almost stole the silver plate from me.

What went wrong wasn't obvious. Earlier travelling in Morocco everything seemed perfect. The magic was in slipping out of time. No landlords, no waiting for you to phone, my love. The air was filled with spice, roast lamb, mysterious music, the delicate odour of pigeon pie. From our hotel room we heard an Arab kid with a knife offer to make a rich woman tourist high for a price. We laughed as his voice mocked her under the arch of the starry sky (twas in life before feminism). I loved our mornings. Honey and the smell of turkish coffee in the huge café at Poco Soco. With the passing donkeys and men in felt hats and beautiful djelabahs obscuring our view of the rich American junkies on the other side, I wrote a poem:

the music of your tongue
slides between my lips
the tongue of your sandal
between my toes
glides through the grass in the orange grove
there has been a communist purge
a dead scorpion lies upturned
on the road to the fortress

Then we were heading northeast across the desert. After a day-and-a-half the train rolled into flowered vineyards, then the city of Algiers. In a lighted square, a white-clothed man with a thin dog leaned back playing his flute to lions of stone. Stepping off the train, a plainclothes cop arrested us. It was midnight. He led us out under the Arabian arches of the station. Saying it was for our own protection. Because the streets at night are dangerous. God, I thought, somehow they're onto the fact we're into heavy politics back in Montréal. What if they find the poem with the word 'communist' in my purse? Now I've really blown it.

The police station was plastered with pictures of missing children. Beautiful girls and boys of all ages. Probably sold to prostitution. That's racist. They let us spread our sleeping bags in the same cell. When in the morning they said: 'You can go now,' my love I was so relieved it seemed that anything was possible. So at a fish supper in a fort restaurant on the middle corniche where Algerian freedom fighters had daringly resisted the French, I said: 'You're right to be against monogamy. As long as we trust each other anything's okay.' Through the open window I saw a beautiful brown man, naked from the chest up. He was looking in, holding a fish net. As if he'd emerged from the sea. 'Anyway,' I added, 'the couple is death for women.' You smiled beautifully with your wonderful soft lips. We headed north. In the mirror of a hotel room in Hamburg you took a self-portrait.

Everything was perfect.

Except, at Ingmar's, your mother's boyfriend's winter house on the Baltic, something started going wrong. That particular morning, I must have been dreaming. Because lying back I saw a face looking through a window, smiling. Vines around its neck. Glistening as though it had risen from the sea. Only outside a slow brown river ran. It was the city. Pink lights on tall white buildings. Red and yellow streets. I woke up to a winter morning. Shadows of noir et blanc. Smell of coffee in a china cup. Bluish tile cooker reaching to the ceiling, Northern European style. Yes, everything was perfect. So why at that precise moment did I get up, open the cooker's little brass door, and throw the photos of your former lovers in the fire? Just as you came in the door.

Your silence left me confused. All that European retenue across the winter room. Then the Modigliani print on the wall behind the golden strands of your hair reminded me I needed a man like you to learn of politics and culture. I'd have to try harder. Thank God, despite my error, our days continued to be wonderful. Walking white streets eating almond-cream buns. The falling snow giving an air of harmony. Only under that blanket of perfection (we were a beautiful couple, everybody said so) the warmth seemed threatened. As if I couldn't handle the happiness. Secretly the darkness of the closet beckoned. I wanted to sink down among the silence of your coats. (Good wool lasts forever.) Your mother, turning her head from a conversation with her son, said to me: 'Comment est ta famille?' I saw the smokestacks of Sudbury. Although we lived nowhere near them. And Her emaciated face sitting on the verandah. 'Fine,' I answered smiling broadly as if I didn't understand the question.

The feminist nemesis was, the more I felt your love the harder it was to breathe. In Hamburg, when the subway stopped between two stations and the lights went out, I began to sweat. Pins and needles pricked my chest so much I wanted to grab your sleeve and say: 'Help please.' But hysteria is not suitable in a revolutionary woman. Thank God a winter-shocked unemployed Syrian immigrant started to bark. His family gathered round him laughing nervously. Eyeing back the fishy stares of other passengers as if it were a joke. As if it were a joke. My fear of crowds at demonstrations was harder to conceal. Although you'd have been initially forgiving. Because you did say paranoia in new politicos is normal. Given how scary it is to become conscious of the way the system really works. Anyway, following that little blowup at Gdansk, when we went to a local march in solidarity, I thought I heard the press of soldiers' feet behind us. Someone yelled 'to the church, to the church!' My love the crowd was barrelling down so heavily, that when they closed the huge oak door I was out and you were in. How could you have let it happen? How?

It wasn't the right question.

The peace in a foreign place was visiting your grandmother. Behind the winter-spring light she stood in her embroidered apron. I said: 'Hers is the last generation before occidental cultural homogenization, dominated by America.' You looked up, interested. Just then your cousin came into the room. Behind her glasses I detected an infinite sadness. 'Gertrude's dead,' she said. 'We think she killed herself because of Lenz. He was having an affair.'

I quickly checked the woman in the mirror over the mantel. She had straight bangs and a well-cut raincoat. It couldn't happen to her. Although I'd have to play it careful now, given how weird I felt. Maybe the trick was to sit straight in my chair (like a European woman), carefully modulating my voice when we disagreed so as not to sound aggressive. You hated a lack of harmony. Unfortunately, my old self-conscious laugh came creeping back. Especially after your high school girlfriend came for a visit. Watching the two of you dance over the Marienbad squares, with her head in that safe place under your chin, I felt like screaming.

Suddenly you grew cooler. Wound up as I was, I didn't see at once that I was spoiling things by trying too hard. Not until I read about the German guy they wrote of in the paper. He wanted a driver's licence more than anything in the world. Due to the fact he'd stayed home on the farm to take care of the folks and needed a way out. Just to make sure he wouldn't fail, he practised in the back field for several years. Then he passed the test without a hitch. The tragedy was that driving home down a country road he hit a girl. In the dark and pouring rain she seemed dead, so he buried her in the stream bed. Incriminating evidence must stay below the surface. After that he'd try harder when he hit them, sometimes backing up and having several other goes, before sending the young women who happened to be walking on the road to their final repose in the sand under the little river.

I've got to get control. Lying with my legs up I see the whole picture in my head. As infinite as unsullied snow. Then a man walks over it in an iron runnered sled. The hard knocks of realism. The dark arpeggios on the radio blend with the sirens outside. Janis is singing: *'Don't you know when you love somebody it's so precious / your beauty could never be had / ah / cheaply.'* If someone comes I'll turn it off. So no one can say: 'You're stuck in the past. In his photos of Morocco; in his images of love.'

That's what Marie said once. Her exact words were: 'Il faut choisir. Car une obsession est une hésitation au point d'une bifurcation.' We were sitting in Figaro's Café, ca 1977, looking at a picture of your other woman. My alabaster cheek against her olive one.

The unfortunate thing is, Janis just happened to come on the air this afternoon when Marie was here. Singing: *Oh baby take a little piece of my heart.* Probably reinforcing the impression I was still living in my own soap opera. With an irritated rattle of her silver Cartier bracelets, Marie reached over and turned it down. Through the partly open bathroom door I watched to make sure her Grecian profile didn't look towards me and say: 'Pour moi ta vie prend les airs d'une tragédie.'

She already said that once. A beautiful summer evening, and I'd just come up the sidewalk in my red flowered skirt. Holding out some sparkling cider and a rose for her. She, standing in the doorway, said, smiling: 'Tu as les petits yeux pétillants, pétillants, pétillants.' Then her face darkened and she showed me a scientific astrological analysis of how women with my birth date often finish tragically. The example was Janis, born on the same day. Dead of an overdose. I said, 'yeah, but she died famous.' Sepia, what scared me was the fatality in Marie's eyes. As if she knew something terrible would happen. I could only think, my love, that it was in regards to you. (We were still together.) So I added nonchalantly: 'Anyway, to the victor belongs the spoiler.'

I'm sorry my love. You were a new man who tried. I just wish you hadn't always spread yourself so thin. At the time it was hard to argue. For when I said: 'Charity begins at home,' you said: 'That isn't communist. What interests us is collective life.' And I could hardly deny the veracity of your statement. The only solution was to find another way to pose the question. Marie said: 'Nous sommes des femmes de transition. En amour, il nous faut éviter la fusion. Evidemment, this leaves a woman pretty empty. I see no other thing to do but write.' I knew what she meant. Putting one word ahead of another on the page gives a feeling of moving forward. I started thinking of the novel I would do.

To get in the mood, when I get out of this tub I think I'll go to that artists' café. The young men sit there every day in black leather jackets and head bands, watching the leaves blow across the street. The bubbles coming from the coffee machine warm the cockles of a single woman. Have to be careful what to wear. In case I meet you and the green-eyed girl. No. The trick is not to be defeatist. Inside the café the smell of coffee is encouraging. A lesbian sings of love in a telephone booth. Her voice rings above the clatter of dishes. This morning an artist was screaming: 'Those fuckers didn't give me a grant.' He meant the government. He was pounding the table with his left hand. Before smiling to himself and drawing circles on his movie program. Outside an old woman was rubbing her stomach as if hungry. He flicked his cigarette at her. It stuck on the orange neon sculpture advertising the work of another painter. She threw back her toothless head and laughed.

My little room is so quiet now. You can almost hear the snow falling on the sidewalk. I'll just turn on the radio. Tonight they're doing that retrospective of women singers, maybe Bessie, Edith, Janis. All their biographies end badly. That won't happen to the heroine of my novel. She was pretty sure of that when (at 25) she climbed off the bus from Sudbury. The smoke hung stiff in the cold sky. At Place Ville Marie she found the French women so beautiful with their fur coats and fur hats under which peep their powdered noses. If anybody asked, she'd say she wanted a job, love, money. The necessary *accoutrements* to be an artist. She immediately rented a bedsitter. Stepping off the Métro that night and turning a corner, she saw the letters FLQ screaming on an old stone wall. Dripping in fresh white paint. Climbing the stairs to her room she knew she'd come to the right place. She just needed some friends. She started looking in the downtown bars, working east to St Denis. Then up The Main. It took a couple of years.

My love, those pictures you took of us on the Lower Main marked the start of my new era. In them I look so happy, so free. Even the dilapidated bars in the background have this silver glow. We're walking from the Lower Main north towards the Upper, your camera clicking all the way. You take one of a guy at the corner of Ste Catherine pissing in the wind. I remember wondering if it felt good. In front of the Lodeo some

English junkies I'd seen hanging around the art galleries wait for a fix. The next shot shows me explaining how artists from rich minorities like les anglais du Québec need marginal lives in order to feel relevant. My black-gloved hand gesturing in the air. You nod, interested, backing up the street, your eye trained on me through the lens. We enter the Cracow Café. The women have pale faces and dark coats over their shoulders.

I could start the novel here. At the Cracow Café, but a little earlier. Just before we met (ca 1973). I felt something stir in me as soon as I walked in. You were sitting under a Polish poster drinking coffee from a thick cup. Lennon glasses on your pretty nose. From the end of every booth a wooden hand beckoned clients to hang up their coats. You had the sweetest smile I'd ever seen on a man. My first thought was this was exactly what I wanted. You and the others sitting there in wire glasses and smoking handrolled cigarettes. Obviously involved in some heavy intellectual discussion. Then the usual moment of doubt when a person naturally draws up a litany of why she'll never rate. No class. Because in Lively a retired mining foreman is something but with an intellectual like you it would be less than nothing. At the time I wasn't political enough to know of your attraction to the working class.

Anyway, I decided to act confident. Aided by the fact that at that moment the door burst open and some hookers came in. They had snowflakes on their hair and eyebrows. To keep warm one of them was dancing wildly. Left foot over right. Until she saw you had your eye on me. She stopped and stared angrily from under her wide pale brow. Very French. And I noticed she had middle-class skin. Therefore no hooker, just one of your socialist-revolutionary comrades dressed up to help organize the oppressed and exploited women of The Main.

'Possessiveness reifies desire,' called a girl with green eyes to her from the next table. So young I hadn't seen her. 'Right on,' I shouted. What did I have to lose? My last lover was a journalist who wouldn't take off his earphones. And his sheets were full of crumbs. The fake hooker cut her losses quicker than I could have. By lighting a Gauloise and launching into a political analysis of prostitution and the city administration. No doubt the better to get your attention. But I was so busy noting the exquisite beauty of her French brow, wide lips and dimple on the chin that I failed to see, my love, how you were smiling at her as sweetly as you smiled at me.

We get up to go. Or at least I do and you follow. This was an essential moment. Outside in the fog we can hear the gulls calling from the harbour. The cold wind cuts. We start walking. The smell of cappuccino is wafting from some restaurant. I love the smell of coffee.

We're on rue Notre Dame. Maybe you're testing my revolutionary potential for going against the system. Because you say, smiling: 'Let me teach you how to fish in a junk shop.' In a display window your hand sweeps away the ropes of pearls. There, on a plaster chest, a purple amethyst. 'Yours,' you say, slipping it in my pocket. Outside you pin it on my sweater. My guilty grin is due to the voice of an old woman behind us in the fog. Someone has snatched her purse. 'Monsieur le policier dit que quand ils sont en uniforme, les gens se privent de faire des mauvais coups,' she says squeakily to her friend. 'Mais quand ils sont pas habillés …' We can hardly see her. But we know she's under some sort of statue. Someone else giggles nervously. The old woman's voice again:

'Tu ris comme une bonne soeur.'

The lens sweeps down the stone steps leading from the chalet towards a street opening bulblike into the mountainside. A grey woman stands up, pushing away her bed of pine boughs. Her hair is silver. Her stockings are stained. Her skirt is a filthy undeterminable colour of suede. She starts walking towards The Main, hugging a fence along a demolition pit. DOWN WITH GENTRIFICATION says the graffiti. She turns the corner.

24

The narrow street curves gently along a row of red brick flats. In some cases the paint on the doors is peeling off. Those with new cedar windows were recently bought by politically progressive university professors. The grey woman heads toward an empty lot and sits down on a cement block. WAIKIKI TOURIST ROOMS, CHAMBRES AVEC CUISINE says a blinking sign.

On the bottom floor to the left, I'm lying in the bath. Watching how in the green five o'clock shadow the conflicting patterns on the rug and sofa dim. With the television flickering in the corner beyond the half-open bathroom door. It could be a scene from an old Hitchcock movie. For this is the 80s, but there is a terrible nostalgia for the past. People are buying those 50s lacquered tables with round corners for their kitchens. The couple is also back in the form of the new woman and the new man. Except us, my love. Because sinking below the line of pain the way I did after we broke up (spring of 79) then reconciled last winter, nearly drove me crazy. I wrote in the black book: *One night a little tipsy and we're together again. I love you but there's no spontaneous outpouring of the warmth I need so much. I drink. I want to take pills and run away. As-tu vraiment peur que je te mange, comme dit Marie?* A little later, we had to break up again.

Shhh. Watch the depression. The solution is not to be burdened, as an F-group comrade told me back in 76. When I got drunk and confessed to him I couldn't handle it when the girl with the green eyes put one hand on my arm and the other on your bum. As if she were the shock centre through which passed our love. We were in Vancouver. Nature was so beautiful with the hibiscus blossoms blooming loudly. I wrote in the black book: *Olympic Vacation, July 23. Arrived by train. The end of a long black corridor. Now I know joy is what I'm looking for. Learn to laugh. No matter what the circumstances being burdened only makes things worse. Don't be such a Protestant.* At the time we were sitting in some wysteria eating a salmon a comrade had lifted from a fish vendor. In the photo I had a nasty frown between my eyes because of trying to explain why it was wrong to steal from the little guys. The comrade answered: 'Under capitalism, you get it while you can. It's sure as hell none of them is going to give any of us anything.' From a transistor on the grass Janis's voice rose up seconding the motion. *In this world / if someone comes along / he gonna give you the love and affection / I say get it while you can....*

Actually I feel fine as long as no one disturbs my peace. A knock at the door really makes me tense. After all it could be anything. The welfare lady looking for a reason to take my cheque from me. 'Do you live alone? We hear you have a boy-friend?' And I'd say just to get her, 'Nope, a woman.' God I hope this place isn't tapped like the one on Esplanade. With the RCMP listening in on every conversation. Of course it isn't.

I'm probably just upset due to Marie's visit. Six months' absence and she walks in as if it were nothing. Being a woman who never looks back. Maybe that's what Janis meant by it's all the same goddamned day. Going with the flow. That québecoise I overheard in the Artists' Café had the right attitude. 'It's over,' she told her friend.

'Oh yeah?' her friend responded from across the table. 'Depuis quand?'

'Depuis un an.'

'Oh I hadn't noticed. No bitterness?'

'Non, pourquoi?'

My love I would have liked to be that way. The better to save me from embarrassing moments like that time all we women comrades were sitting somewhere. A woman's party, I think. Twas near the end of the reconciliation and it was important to be cool. The girl with the green eyes came in looking sad and skinny. With a shock I noticed her hair was cut and with the side part she exactly resembled your mother. That's how I began to think she was trying to have an affair with you. 'Women get old,' I told her, 'so they won't be attractive to their sons.'

It was a stupid thing to say. But I was trying to control the darkness so I wouldn't do something terrible. In my pocket was the blowup of that article where Prince Charles, in announcing his engagement, said by way of explanation: 'Diana will keep me young.' I was thinking of pinning it on your door. Clandestinely, because when you saw it you wouldn't find it funny. The idea came as I got up one silver morning. The snow was melting so fast a Quebec poet had written 'Time is slush' and printed it in the paper. You were coming to get the little Chilean girl we were looking after (her parents being illegal in the country). But what to my surprise did I see, as I peeked out the window of the flat on Esplanade, but the girl with the green eyes waiting on the sidewalk. Her smile was surprisingly warm. Still it couldn't have been easy. The eyes looked small and swollen as if crying. And the mouth stretched, almost, in the pale face. I saw the large penis slip between our lips. I felt the soreness of the jaws after awhile. This was just before that beautiful April scene where the two of you walked up the street like lovebirds. So when you came up for little Marilù and I asked you how come the girl with the green eyes was also at the bottom of the stairs so early in the morning, you said: 'We're all friends, we three, so why are you acting suspiciously?'

I said, the words sticking painfully in my throat: 'Does friendship include uh sex?'

And you said: 'We're friends. And you'd know more if you asked less.'

Out the March window I checked her face once more. She looked scared she wouldn't win. Just like I was probably looking then, in that last period of our love. The same face exactly. Except I knew my star was falling and hers was rising. That's a defeatist way to see the picture. Actually, my love, when you said you were just friends, I believed you. For people were saying she was a dyke. Besides creeping through a corner of my mind was that funny little slogan: 'To the victor belongs the spoiler.' I should have said that to the shrink from McGill who said: 'We need to find the darkness in you that makes you tolerate such a situation. A woman who loves herself doesn't put up with a man who deprives her of affection.'

Instead I reminded her for the nth time a political woman has to be open. I repeated once more the problem with therapy lies in its lack of social analysis. She listened as I pointed out how in coming up the winding oak stairs to her office I'd noticed the panelled walls of the English-speaking school of social work forbade protest with signs that said: 'NO POSTERING; PAS D'AFFICHAGE.' They had the same signs except only in French and pinned on the cement block walls at the University of Quebec. But over there no one paid attention. The place was covered with graffiti. QUÉBECOISES DEBOUTTE. SOCIALISME ET INDÉPENDANCE. LE QUÉBEC AUX OUVRIERS. People were freer then.

The shrink, a jolly Aries with a round grey Beatle haircut, asked: 'Is there any more you want to say before you leave?'

I decided to tell her about the dream. Because there were three birds but I couldn't see the third bird's face. Try as I might. It was very frustrating. The first one was a nightingale, very modest, sitting in the long grass in the grey dawn singing a beautiful song representing infinite poetic possibilities for the future. The second was attached to the first by a string. It flew up into the blue sky where the world could see. A painted bird, trendily attractive, chattering madly. But its song was very thin. The third was sitting on a tree with its back to us. Fully developed and a beautiful singer. But we couldn't see what kind it was.

The shrink said, 'Gail, I think it's pretty obvious, don't you? The first one is the darkness, the night in you we talked about earlier. Still it's very beautiful when not obfuscated by the image of the second, the painted bird you are choosing to show the world.'

'Very deep,' I said sarcastically. 'Anybody who has been a sympathizer of the surrealist movement can tell you how to read manifest dream content. The point is we have to create new images of ourselves even if at first they're superficial, in order to move forward. Otherwise we're sitting back there in the grey dawn. But what's the latent content? What I want to know is who that third bird is?'

28

'Well,' she said, 'when you do maybe you will have come full circle. You say the third bird is 'fully developed.' I presume that means having transcended the two others. The third bird is your answer to the future.'

I guess dream time is like train time. No line between night and day, yesterday and tomorrow. Waking up periodically on that trip to Vancouver, it could have been a dream. First the fat blonde woman from Keewatin in the powder blue pant suit drinking with the boys all night. Yet staying fresh as a daisy. She'd even left her children home and wasn't worried. Often when I opened my eyes she'd be telling another joke about some Indian or a hunting story or something. And once when I awoke a storm was blowing and suddenly out of the forest in a flash of lightning I saw written on a huge stone: 'With schizophrenia you're never alone.' We were going through reserve country.

In the dark I thought how I'd like to capture that loneliness and write it in a novel. But it was already too late because the train was out of the forest and going through a giant field of car wrecks.

Car Wrecks and Bleeding Hearts

Clarity. The trick is to tell a story. Keeping things in the same time register. I go with you to Europe. There our love starts. Subsequently I get involved in heavy politics. Then we're the attractive left-wing couple returning home from abroad. Clothes perfectly cut yet appropriately dressed down: high boots, purple blouse, short leather skirt. The comrades are anti-couple. But in the Bistro they can't get over how good I look. 'You've really changed,' says one. 'Les femmes rouges sont toutes belles,' says another. The marble tables are laden with beer. Through the smoke I see the comrade's pockmarked face in the mirror. The hypocrite! Still, my love, I wonder do I look good because your arms keep me from bleeding all over town in search of love? Like I was before.

Oh Mama why'd you put this hole in me?

Stop. This is the city, 1980. A single raindrop squeezes out of the sky. Cut the melodrama, two lesbians told me back in 77. They were in that crazy café singing of love in the telephone booth. So beautiful, so free. One had a thick lock of brown curls down her neck. The other with tiny fingers and red lips. When she talked her voice was that of a happy bird. I was writing it all in the black book, looking, grant it, kind of sad. She said, mocking: 'We hope the heroine of that story isn't a heterosexual victim. Il y en a trop dans le monde.'

What did they take me for? Of course I know nostalgia can't penetrate a real city. Maybe it seemed right as country & western coming out of a false-fronted restaurant near Sudbury. A girl was crossing a dusty village street. All decked out in a red velvet suit. Waiting for the small blue dot to come over the bridge. Larger and larger. But the two-toned blue Ford didn't come. Mrs. Callaghan was hanging clothes on the line. Having a hard time raising her arms over her head because she was pregnant. Out of the door came the hairdresser son with his girlfriend whom he'd just done platinum blonde. 'Have you seen D (the boy with the blue Ford)?' asked the girl worriedly. 'No,' they said, trying to look innocent. On the radio Hank Williams was singing: *The news is out all over town / you're running round / I know I should leave, but then I just can't go / you win again.* In the purple dusk the girl felt scared. Albeit a corner of her mind rejoiced at relief from boredom. Coming up to the city she quickly adopted black clothing as a sign of urban sophistication. The next step was to cut the melodrama.

Black plus white is the colour of the 8os. (Like that winter afternoon of our love?) Marie in her immaculate white silk on the sofa of my bed-sitter this afternoon was a portrait of the decade. The vermilion lips on powdered skin a Greek mask covering the face of the 7os feminist. Don't be moralistic. It's the heart that counts. Continuing my ablutions I could see, through the open bathroom door, her glance fix once more on the dirt and grease accumulating over the stove. Turning to me (at last) she says, almost angrily: 'What are you going to do?'

I turn off the water, the better to hear. 'Do? I don't know. Write a novel maybe.'

Outside the black sneaker boots and black pants of a famous Montréal modern dance troupe go by the window.

'You've been saying that for years. Fais quelque chose.'

I could do without the greasepaint. But what a mouth she has. Back when I cut the profile of a winner, we kissed on her bed. I was lying on top of her soft breasts. Then she pulled up her white nightshirt and pulled down her panties. But I rolled off. Swallowing the pain, she rolled a joint with her tanned fingers. It was the pot falling on the floor that gave her the energy to move forward. As if two negatives could make a positive, she stood up and said energetically: 'Je ferais le ménage demain.' As she ushered me toward the door. 'Bonsoir,' she said, turning towards me her beautiful gallic profile. I went down the iron staircase. Under it the initials FLQ were fading on the brick wall. There was a Bar Salon on the corner –

'Rends-toi intéressante si tu veux avoir des amis,' Marie adds.

As she stands up and moves towards the television, her expensive skirt falls around her thick calves. I'm not jealous, but a dress like that you can only buy on $40,000 a year. Maybe she sold out by going to work at the film board. That's unfair. Bitterness will get you nowhere. Besides high salaries and job security are the fruit of progressive union militance.

Tis nearly November. From the mountain top the Black tourist watches the field of car wrecks below the skyscrapers. The old woman stands up from her bench and starts walking along the cement river bank towards the city centre. At some point she turns and takes the street that runs up the middle. The Main. Her stockings are stained. Behind a postage-stamp window a light shines under a bushel. Sepia, I know that's silly, but I can't find the word. In the dictionary they call it a rudimentary penis. Ohhhhh dream, rising sap is the stuff of art....

Out the window that trendy dance troupe goes by in the other direction. They walk leaning forward, flat-footed. Like they were nearly falling off the world. In the Blue Café I heard someone say they dance as if the couple is back, except there is tremendous violence between men and women. Their choreographer is supposed to be brilliant. I saw him go into the lobby of the Cooper Building where artists live and where in the mornings the girls sun themselves on the front steps in black high heels and net stockings. He was wearing a white shirt and black pants and stood weighing an apple in his hand. Later the young genius' head could be seen at a fifth-storey window. It is said there is nothing in his room but a bed and a computer.

Through the bathroom door my little room looks overstuffed. But I like my tub. Oh froth stay warm now Marie's gone. Maybe we'll get somewhere. Looking at those feminists in the restaurant the other day who said: 'We feel sorry for you, how long has it been since you've had a man?' I made a terrible grimace. My lip trembled in self-pity. One had madonna hair and big earrings. Although really it was all an act for I was thinking: A woman needs a man like a fish needs a bicycle. I saw that slogan at a demonstration. Out loud I answered sweetly, 'Ah never mind that, it doesn't matter.' But they were women and could see the edge on my tongue.

Oh my big mouth. My hungry mouth. Mother why did you make this hole in me? Those were my thoughts on the way down from Sudbury. Actually, I was locked in a room in the Ottawa bus station. Old tiles and oak panel doors. Later they tore it down. 'Do you speak French?' said someone among the noise of toilets whooshing.

'Where's Daddy?' A little girl's voice.

'In the men's. Don't do that or you'll get a slap.

'You'll get swallowed.'

I put my finger on mine, too, thinking of the last guy I'd seen in that God-forsaken mining town. He was a visiting creative writing professor from Ottawa University. We were in his back seat, parked behind the Sudbury arena. Really going to it, when suddenly he said (as I tried to pull him down on top of me): 'Stop. I feel like I'm going to drown.' And HE PULLED BACK. Should have known from the start. He'd kiss me with his tousled golden head. Then I'd put my arms around him. And suddenly he'd do this prissy gayblade sidestep to avoid my lips. Made my stomach so tense it hurt. That's why in the washroom I said: 'Oh Mama why'd you put this hole in me.' Thank God nobody heard.

No. Cut the pessimism. In the words of a male writer I know pessimism just leads to a lot of images going nowhere. He was sitting in Harvey's-on-the-Main. The place was full of writers because the general insecurity of the economic situation was creating sympathy among progressive intellectuals for the unemployed quarter of the population. He'd come to watch the 12-year-old hookers. Probably wondering where his daughter was. Out loud he said: 'When I'm 55 I'll have a boring office job or be sitting in some dive.'

'Who's pessimistic?' I asked grinning, only too glad to point out to a former leader of the revolutionary organization that he was in contradiction. In the Harvey's mirror I was wearing a red sweater. Beside us was the reflection of an older hooker, her front teeth missing. She was combing her hair. Her white laminated boots came over the knees of her bulging jeans, the crotch of which was vaguely pee-stained. On the sidewalk the rain fell in big drops. A kid with a few pimples was trying to solicit. His jeans were perfect over his tight hips. Every time a driver slowed down he ran toward it. When the driver shook his head, the kid showed greater and greater panic.

'That kid better watch out or he's going to get picked up by the cops,' said the writer as if he knew. He added, looking tiredly at me: 'I meant cut the pessimism in your writing. Pessimism is the failure of past illusions. Even feminists agree on the necessity of writing forward to a positive solution. Obviously in real life it's more complicated. The right-wing leaders of the world are death-stalkers. Pour nous il n'y aura pas de lendemains qui chantent. We have to climb off our dreams and enjoy the little things of life.'

He's right, my love. I'm glad for what we had. Before you put your hands on my face nobody ever touched me like that. I used to sit close to Her on the verandah. It was very hot. The mosquitoes buzzed around my neck. The air was so intense with heat it became a screen. Reflecting the bleeding hearts growing by the sidewalk bigger and bigger.

I said: 'Mom, I'm scared.'

She answered (without even looking): 'Then get down on your knees and pray to the Lord.'

After your kiss on the linoleum and one thing led to another,

I noticed how your fingers curled like a child's against my
cheek. In perfect satisfaction. I'd never known harmony like
that. It was peace in a foreign place. The warm air blowing
through the curtains on St Denis St. brought me to my senses.
Coward that I am I almost said: 'Here comes spring with its
rapier.'

In the telescope, the grey woman stands by the fish shop gath-
ering herself for the leap. She has been rubbing her two dimes
over the herring pail. Now she puts her muddy galoshes on the
side of the pail and gathers her skirts above her spattered legs.
   'Get rid of that female impersonator,' shouts the shopkeeper.
His name is Nikki. From the fish shop to the Waikiki Tourist
Rooms is only a few blocks. Two up The Main, a block west on
Ave. des Pins and two along Sewell St. which curves gently.
Walking in the wind along the construction fence this morning
I noticed the QUÉBEC INDÉPENDANT graffiti had been
painted over by STARVING DOGS EAT SHIT. In the light,
Sewell St. leading up to my cozy home looked like an excerpt
from a Swedish movie. The one where the clocks have no faces.
Wild Strawberries.
   Oh froth, your warm faucet's spurting warmly over my uh
small point. Maybe strawberry is the word I'm looking for.
Damn. Now Dr. Schweitzer is on the radio talking about the
lack of fresh organs for transplants. On account of the new seat-
belt legislation which has resulted in fewer fatal accidents.
Shhh. Focus on something else. Yes. Mon beau bébé. Was that
you I saw standing in the park the other day? With your knee
bent holding the soccer ball between your legs? Like those busi-
nessmen squeezing their briefcases on the train? Your beautiful
bronze skin gleaming above and below your short shorts, which
could scarcely contain your ponderous member. Some girls
passed wearing bright red lipstick and haltertops. One of them
stopped to stare at the goods. I could hear her say: 'To hell with

women's liberation. What I want is a nice piece. Something to hold on to. Kinda fills up the emptiness, you know what I mean?' They all laughed.

I laughed also. Because, Sepia, even feminists have their needs. What was it again that Marie said this afternoon? Oh yeah, she said (first taking a cigarette between her tapered fingers): 'We have to transcend being women of our generation. Because having both square dancing and rock 'n roll on Saturday nights confused our identities. Not to mention feminism a little later. On dirait que certaines n'en ont pas fait la synthèse (the huge brown eye rolled quite far in my direction). Maybe younger women have it easier.'

I said nothing. Watching Marie smoke, I wanted to ask for one, too. Then she'd have had to come in here and bend over the tub to give it to me. Close up her skin has a special sheen, the pores so fine you can hardly see them. The way she looks pale or dark depending on the fashion is amazing. Or maybe she's just pale now due to overworking. Using herself up without thinking about her health. First off in the morning, three cups of strong coffee and cigarettes to work up a buzz. Then she just keeps going on nervous energy, standing very straight and forgetting she's hungry until she falls into bed at night. I'm the type who saves herself too much.

No, I think that trendy pale effect has to be makeup. Either it's plastered on now or it was back in 77 when her skin looked darker. If I could just remember what colour she was under the tan line of the mauve panties that time we were lying side by side on her bed. When she put her mouth on my uh widow's beak saying 'Just a little taste. Mmm salty. Now you reciprocate.' Embarrassed though I was I said: NO. After which she smoked a joint thoughtfully, then ushered me to the door.

Puis entre nous il y eut un froid. Making me feel weird the next time I saw her. Twas Janis' birthday and 30 below. I went out to the steam bath anyway, because Tuesday is the only day for women. In the 20s, the wives of Jewish shopkeepers went on Tuesdays, later the newer Mediterranean arrivals. Now on Tuesdays it's the feminists who come. The floor has those turn-of-the-century black-and-white tiles just like my little bathroom here at the Waikiki Tourist Rooms. We take showers then sit in the steam room flicking each other with cedar branches. I was flicking a white-skinned Virgo from France. Her back got quite red when I hit it. Anyway, looking up from my task I spied Marie. Lying stark naked beside a beautiful woman on a narrow couch only wide enough for one. Bonjour, I said, trying to sound nonchalant. Later in the shower the soap kept slipping from my grasp. Because I knew they were watching the water fall over my skinny shoulders and the slightly crooked back. Relax, I said. Fais pas ton anglaise.

To calm down I sat in a darkened corner until the Russian masseuse could take me. She was slow, having gained weight and become red in the face. So on the narrow couches between the mirrors and the lockers, women began massaging one another. This was my chance. As soon as Marie, with her frank thick calves and full but not pendulous breasts, the profile of a beautiful brunette, stopped talking to that stunning auburn woman whose reflection I could see in the mirror, I'd walk over and offer to massage her.

Malheureusement, les choses se gâchaient. For suddenly the huge masseuse with her red face was there screaming at the women bending tenderly over their friends: 'You haff no right. You haff no right. I'm the masseuse. You give me twelve dollars or you haff to leave.' Of course we ignored her. Except there came the softly whispered rumour that this was the night the cops were going to raid the lesbian establishments. We left in a hurry, half-dressed. Outside our hair froze immediately. Later we learned it was Mrs. Simka the owner's wife who started the story.

She was a smart woman.

From the mountaintop, the Black tourist turns his telescope. The grey woman sloshes through a yellow puddle and climbs some outside stairs. Her sister died there. Twas the novocaine before Christmas. She was allergic but failed to tell the welfare dentist. Farther down, the tracks of an iron runnered sled reflect off a low green window. On the radio Edith Piaf is singing: *Je ne regrette rien.* So beautiful, so sad. She was a free woman. Singing her pain to make a story out of the chaos.

I could do that in the novel. Of course, in a story, you tell, not sing. Starting at the Sudbury bus station and moving forward. The music's playing. I'm wearing a brown-and-white checked coat. A little hicky but good quality. She always taught me to put the best foot foward. In that early photo even though Daddy's still an ordinary miner, I look like a prince's daughter. A handknit coat and matching beret over white dress and fluffy slip. He's crouching there beside me. Looking so proud. I can't help it. Even though the camera's about to click I start jumping up and down in ecstasy shouting Daddy Daddy. All the adults are laughing.

Anyway, I'm standing in the Sudbury bus station. Unable to help smiling at how all the guys came sniffing round the minute they heard I was leaving town. For one last go. A man in moccasins was singing the French language is dangerous. The bus smelled of sick. Excited as I was, I kept getting up to pee. After awhile we went through reserve country. Millions of pines leaning crazily over the horizon. On the other side of the forest was a giant field of car wrecks. We passed a canal. And back yards with frozen sheets on clotheslines strung from sagging tin sheds. Then came the skyscrapers. It was snowing. The bus station smelled of coffee. 'Come for lunch,' said the nun sitting beside me. She was concerned about the city's bad influences on young women. I imagined baked tomatoes with soda crackers. 'No thanks,' I said. 'I'm a job hunter.' Sort of joking. To tell you the truth I didn't know where to look. Soon my feet were wet with slush. 'How about a little drink first?' I said to myself. I went through a bar-salon swinging door. Through the window rose the mansions on the mountainside. Topped by a brightly-coloured cross.

'What's that?' I asked the bar-salon waitress.

'That's where they shit on us from.'

On you, I thought. As for me I'm going straight to the top.

Sorry, Sepia. That was in life before politics. Before that grey winter day, when I entered the the Cracow Café. And looked around at the intense faces, the dark shirts, the wire-rimmed glasses. Behind me in the entrance a blond hooker with dark circles under her eyes nervously dialed the phone. She looked so desperate and her knees kept sagging as if, unless she got an answer, she was going to sink down.

I sat, smiling so hopefully that for some reason you slid out over the torn red plastic seat opposite and slid in the booth beside me. A moment of tension. Then two women sat down facing us. You said, blushing as befits a new man, 'You've stumbled into one of our café discussions on Marxism.' I smiled more, thinking of the last lover with his earphones and filthy sheets. All he ever wanted was to get stoned. What's a lonely woman to do? Listening to your measured words spoken in a European accent I thought: At last, a man who knows how to talk.

You were saying: 'The human race has but two choices, barbarism or Marxist revolution.'

I laughed out loud, nearly hooting (you have to watch things like that with sophisticated people) and said: 'It sounds like you've got religion, the way you're talking.'

Your face got even redder. I noticed your green eyes were spotted, like a tiger's through your rimless glasses. Your voice said: 'Marxism is the ultimate form of realism. Just another tactic for understanding systems.' My father's eyes were spotted, too. Only hungrier. Eyeing me with them after we went berry picking once, he said: 'You're too romantic; you'll have to learn to be more realistic.' I didn't really know what he meant.

Later, my love, taking pictures, when it seemed to me we saw it all the same, I began to think of you as an extra window on the world. Helping me figure out what real is. The green-eyed girl also came to F-group's pre-recruitment briefings to speak on the relationship between dialectic thinking and women's liberation. She said Marxism is the proper view of history, providing it accounts for the needs of women. I was too embarrassed to ask what that implied regarding love. After, she came to my room. In the park downstairs was a demonstration of Québecois and Irish comrades. Their slogans read: DOWN WITH IMPERIALLY-IMPOSED CONSTITUTIONS. Except in French. She came in in an old school tunic (the better to mock her wealthy Argentinian background), smooth legs, pink cheeks and flying cherub curls.

Then we went to a Spanish Café. Her green eyes in her incredible pale coffee skin were as limpid as two pools. I was feeling odd because upstairs there'd been a funny tension between us. Although nobody made a move. Now she raised her small pink fingers in the air and said I wasn't revolutionary material yet because. Flamenco music drowned out her words.

I thought: 'We'll see about that.'

The telescope cuts out a circle. Whitening fast for after midnight tis November. At one edge of the lens, a string of car wrecks. On the other side a low green window where light won't shine until next spring. That's okay. I'm lying in the bath, feeling fine. As long as I can be alone. An artist needs solitude to create. If that Dr. Schweitzer comes on the radio, I'll turn him off. Yesterday he said modern women, despite their freedom, have a great difficulty of personal synthesis. Suffering as we do from terrible restlessness. Due to overly developed expectations in life and love. The pimp. What does he know? It's either happiness (where for a moment the world is your oyster and the possibilities so phenomenal you can't stand it) or unhappiness. The rest of the time it's floating along in the middle enjoying the little consolations. The bath, the warmth, the television in the corner of the room. One thing about the Waikiki Tourist Rooms is they supply everything. A person doesn't have to worry. She can focus on her work.

41

What inhibited me was Marie's visit. For earlier, I'd been sinking into a jazz afternoon at the Blue Café. Very moving. The spoons strung high against long-stemmed glasses. Se-i-i-i-i. Above the winter clatter of dishes the waitress's voice singing in treble broke so you could feel the pain. The café has a blue floor. Over the strains of jazz snippets of conversation. C-cocaine. My eye fell on the straight back of a Sephardic woman. I could tell she was a dancer by the way she kept bending over in ballet stretches. The skin was a particular olive, so different I'm attracted. On the other side of her a younger version of Jagger, smiling vaguely, aware of his charm on women.

I got up to go, concentrating on how to put the whole symphony down on paper. With the heroine a free spirit (although you can taste the fragility of her chances, for self, for love) radiating from the middle of the story. Out in the grey air I walked like a careful drunk, looking neither right nor left so as not to confuse my creative radar. Except what to my dismay do I see in front of the Waikiki Tourist Rooms but Marie? She's standing on the steps. They have artificial turf carpeting. Bright green under the old wooden door with its turquoise paint chipped off. I didn't know what to do. On one hand no one ever comes. But on the other hand I wanted to be alone.

I had to admit, in that black wool coat, 40s style, she was looking really good. I think she got it from an aunt. I open the door. We descend the inside stairs, a little slanting, down to my semi-basement room. True, this place smells slightly greasy. True there's the odour of garbage, faintly. From behind a door, you can hear the voice of that former steno who can't stop talking. Back when she had a job it got so she could hear everything. Earphones on or off, she couldn't help listening. She had to stop eating in restaurants because she could hear every conversation at every single table. *Political situation prostituting fascist referendum wife of Frank's girl's legs mufflers getting expensive four-to-one the Expos under conditions for selling stocks on St James' the church over the bridge at skis in the oracle ha ha that's what you get for being a nose-and-throat man.* Now everything that goes in her ears comes out her mouth. Shrugging it off, I stick my keys in my lock and open my door. Marie looks in. Then she says, fixing me with her sad brown eyes that have kohl around them and dark circles under them:

'Dis-moi pas que c'est ici que tu restes.'

Sepia, that's the tyranny of intimacy. My mother made the same mistake. Always waiting on the verandah after dances at the crossroads back in Lively. Her moon was in Cancer. Once She was stricken, She smelled of soaked Kotex. At night the dogs spread the black napkins over the snow. Anyway, following the love in the parked car, we kids hurried home beetling down the dirt road. The girls in the front seat, the boys in the back. I knew at that speed we'd never make the corner. The wind wobbled on my cheeks. The cows mooed lazily in the cool green grass by the river. *Roll me over in the clover.*

'All I got was a rip in my skirt. Honest Mom.'

But from the verandah She looked at me sadly with brown eyes that were growing a white haze over the pupils. I felt so terrible I couldn't make Her happy, I started planning my departure. When, at dinner, I said 'Montréal' the whole family winced. Then Lucie McVitty, the old maid across the street who watched me coming home at night through her lace curtains, gave me the address of a niece in Westmount. As she handed me the piece of paper torn off Boyd's General Store calendar with the cute little red-cheeked girl biting on an apple, she whispered:

'Watch out, white iris stems fade quickly, when uprooted.' Then she shut the door.

Coming up to the city, it was winter. I straightened and smiled to myself, thinking of freedom. Two hookers were standing on the corner under magnificent Japanese umbrellas outside the bus depot. At least I thought they were hookers. Looking so interesting with their tight jeans and shiny black hair falling over their fur collars. But that was in life before politics. When the wild streak in me failed to see the true degree of sexual exploitation involved when a woman sells her body. One of them was doing a tiny little two-step in order to keep warm. Left foot down twice. Then the right.

'Welcome to Montréal,' I thought, feeling anything was possible. And I crossed the street to a place that said: BAR / RESTAURANT: LICENCE COMPLÈTE. The waitress held her back perfectly straight and her stomach flat under her pale green uniform. As she stretched over to polish the mirror beneath the red signs advertising CUISINE QUÉBÉCOISE: TOURTIÈRE, FÈVES AU LARD, TARTE AU SUCRE, SOUPE AUX POIS, I wondered why French women have better posture. I tried to start a conversation. 'Uh, je cherche un logement. Y en a-t-il dans le coin?' I guess she picked up my English accent, because she answered me resentfully: 'Pour qui tu me prends? Le Journal de Montréal?'

My love, you said I wasn't modern, but you should have seen me then. It's true I took the bus to English Westmount as a temporary measure. The titillating note was what happened just as I stepped off. My nostrils were smarting from the odour of wet fur. Mink, raccoon, muskrat. One guy even had a silver fox hat with the tail still on it. Jane McVitty lived in a brick building that looked like a fort. I rang the bell. As she opened the door and I put my suitcase down on the floor, there was a huge explosion from across the courtyard. Then they interrupted CBC's hockey night in Canada to say the FLQ had blown up the Westmount Armoury. I must have smiled. Back in Sudbury, a couple of striking miners used explosives on a company office when the bosses brought in scabs. At the sound of crackling stone and glass, the faces of everyone in the Ladies And Escorts of the Sudbury Hotel lit up. So I'm standing there I guess with a little smile tickling the corners of my mouth. And Jane's husband Bill stops swirling his scotch in his chilled glass and stares at me aghast. Getting control, I say as sweetly as I can: 'It's only for the night, I'll go tomorrow.'

The next morning I took a walk. Only too happy to do so. Twas April, 1970, and in the wet snow my boots left slushy prints. After fifteen minutes my feet were soaked. Still, walking east on Sherbrooke, I felt so good, so free I started looking for a café where I could sit and write about it. (I was a poet, my love, before I was with you.) There were only chic boutiques in Victorian greystone houses. Fancy rugs, glasses, lingerie in pink and black and purple. There's nothing like a woman with lace next to her skin. Very classy, very French. I passed the Ritz. The suitcase was growing heavy. Suddenly the buildings were lower, sagging even, so they seemed to lean together. On a wall in fresh white paint was written QUÉBEC LIBRE. AMOUR ET ANARCHIE.

I opened the next door. Its sign said La Hutte Suisse. In the semi-darkness waitresses carried huge trays of drafts with their solid arms. The guys in the booths were skinny with tinted glasses. Little beards on pale skin. I could see the titles of reading material spread on the tables, *Le Monde*, *Socialisme québécois*, *Liberté*. I could tell this was a hangout for radical French intellectuals. It felt so good. I sat as near them as I could, trying to make eye contact. In the booth across from me was an English guy, some journalist trying to get a story on the new revolutionary generation of québécois. He really stood out with his short hair and heather-coloured mohair sweater. To the point of cliché. One of the French guys raised his glass, quite aggressive, and shouted VIVE MALCOLM X, VIVE LE FLQ. Everybody laughed. Then he leaned across to the English guy and asked: 'C'est-tu vrai que tu travailles pour le PC?'

'Oui,' says the English guy, looking uncomfortable.

'Le PC, veux-tu dire le Parti Communiste?' Everyone was smirking.

'Non, la Presse Canadienne,' says the English guy. Now he was really blushing. All the others were holding their sides.

I was laughing too as I walked out. The April air was damp with spring and hope. Seeing a For Rent sign on a basement flat, I went down some stairs to look. Through the window, the floor was covered with garbage. I went up the outside stairs anyway and rang for the janitor. 'I can't go down now,' she shouted.

'I'm waiting for a phone call.' A few blocks north, I found another one. It had a mint-green balcony, kind of crooked, where I sat when summer came waiting for Louis. Sepia, I didn't have much choice if I wanted the experience. Because in that particular period québécoise was beautiful, leaving a low premium on English women. Also we had a different relationship to time. Or so it seemed, waiting. He had such a beautiful face, with lips that moved easily with emotion under his clear brown eyes. Generally, it was love in the afternoon. I'd put on my black skirt all ready for the night shift at the wire service where they'd hired me as translator. And drink beer sitting in the wide old-fashioned window cavity. Sometimes he didn't show up for days and the circle of empties joined on the other side of the room. Once he came in and I wanted to say 'you're late.' But he was standing there in perfect jeans and some kind of a soft brown shirt, his words reaching me in a crooked line across the tense grey air of the room.

'Bonjour ma belle, t'es bien belle aujourd'hui. Sit down, I've got something to tell you. Mais écoute-moi. C'est assez drôle ce que j'ai à te raconter. I was filling up my tank at a gas station on the way over. When a woman crosses the street from her apartment building and says: "T'es bien beau, toi. Pourquoi tu ne montes pas avec moi." So I go up there and we make love and just as I'm putting my clothes on her husband comes in and says, "Thank you." He'd been watching through a crack in the door. He gave me $50 for my trouble. We're rich, let's have dinner!'

I laughed, so happy yet so sad. Loving his decadence even if it hurt. He said I just needed to learn some spontaneity. He'd learned his by racing Formula 1's. Because if you're not present every minute, with the speedometer rising like an orgasm (those were his words), you're gone forever. Sitting beside him in his racecar, I admired the way his tight thighs in their well-cut jumpsuit hugged the leather seat on fast curves. Through the slightly opened window, the intoxicating smell of summer dust filled my nostrils. Tentatively I put my hand on his leg. But then lying in the field only a soft-hard point came inside me. In the ecstasy of hay-flowers my singing body couldn't get enough. As if it were being penetrated by a butterfly. He got up and lit an Export A, grumpily. Then he disappeared towards the lot of car wrecks along the field's edge his friend owned for selling parts to car buffs. In the distance you could hear the motors revving on Mont Tremblant's raceway. The field took on that dusk-dark green I saw in a movie once about a murder in a park. *Blowup.* But no matter how hard they looked on that dark grass they couldn't see the body. I threw my shoulders back. Who's scared? This is the city. Far far away from the heat wave magnifying snowdrops and bleeding hearts along Her sidewalk. Recalling the thing She loved, a wedding, and the thing She hated, marriage.

Autumn Leaves

The city. Hot autumn. In an apartment a couple are sitting at a table discussing revolution. Through the open balcony door a warm breath blows a dustball across the floor. Below, a narrow street of two-storey red brick flats culminating in a mountain with a cross on top.

She's one of those attractive 60s-type women with small breasts under her T-shirt, tight jeans and kinky red hair. He smiles at her sweetly although inside he's angry because she's not interested in sex recently. She's frustrated because he leaves his towels on the floor. How can a woman live on the edge if she's constantly saying pick up this, pick up that? Also she doesn't like the way he behaves as a lover. Why should his orgasms always be stronger? In her diary it says: *Before I was with him nothing good really happened to me in matters of love. Now I am cared for. But with all his sexual demands (or is it my jealousy, never wanting him to go out without me?) I never feel free.*

There are dark arpeggios on the radio. With his hand on her knee (she's the creative one) she writes a poem:

Sunday afternoon
with the coffee cup

between my fingers
passe-moi   la bouteille
sec

- - -

on Highway 31 the cars slide by
tri-colour birds are mating in the Easter sky
passe-moi   la bouteille
sec

Oh my love was that really us? With me at the centre and you watching from the margin of the picture. So what went wrong? I mean how did I slip out of focus in your retina? Shhh, cut the nostalgia.

Tis a grey day. As if time has stopped. But you know it hasn't because it just keeps getting greyer and greyer until it's dark. Still for a minute I wondered, because looking out my little window earlier I saw this woman pass. She was wearing an old checked coat and carrying an orange shopping bag. An hour later I looked out again and she was passing in exactly the same place. As if nothing had changed.

Oh, the water's getting cold. I'll have to get out soon. If I can manage just a tickle, it's a sign I'll write the novel. A certain rigidity of the body also precedes explosion. The bigger it is the more likely a woman is to cry after. Tears of joy with that window face watching from the corner. Don't be silly. As I said, the window's turning green. A sort of moss because the sun won't shine on it until the spring.

Now the American president is on the radio. Saying the United States is vastly increasing its nuclear stocks in order to have peace. Who's worried? As a sympathizer of revolution I believe in *les lendemains qui chantent*. Why already a new generation of young men are deploying their progressive feathers in anti-nuclear demonstrations. I met one who got arrested. He had a red pompadour and a pink silk scarf. I wanted to sleep with him but he thought I was too old. We were at a huge rally in the park. Except the city had ploughed the grass under in big furrows so the people couldn't sit down.

After it was over, I walked up the street a little farther. Knowing full well I could have looked better. What a mistake that was. For you my love were standing at your door, smiling tenderly. I loved your mouth. It drew me to you when the rest of your body cut like a knife. And there, by the side of the wonderful new man you are, stood the girl with the green eyes shaking out an anti-nuke sign. The lucky woman, profiting from everything I taught you. Shh, bitterness will get me nowhere. I thought: 'Too bad I'm wearing the olive-green jumpsuit. It's so baggy.' Maybe that is why the eyes of a former woman comrade who saw me at the rally filled with something I couldn't identify. 'Are you happy?' she asked. I didn't answer, knowing what she meant by that was something very traditional (despite her red flag with the white dove on it) – i.e. Do you have a man? Whereas I've found another way to pose the question. Anyway I'm wearing the faded olive jumpsuit so I walk on the shady side of the elm. That way you and the girl with the green eyes cannot see the wrinkles.

'Hello.'

'Hello,' you say, but your body stiffens. She takes your arm supportively. I feel like saying to her SOLIDARITY. The older feminist talking to the younger. Is it true younger women are more relaxed about progressive sexual relations than us? I hear they cut down on romantic expectations. The better not to worry if their lovers fool around. In the dream you slipped out of my arms and into hers. You were dancing to a waltz. The music was Schubert. I was shocked because they were playing something so romantic. Then I saw her laughing at my projection of how she was feeling. Whereas she knew better than to take the music seriously. Yes, she knew what I didn't: that by going through the romantic motions while drastically reducing expectations, a woman's safer. She can live and let live. I knew it too, my love, but I felt so needy.

Stop complaining. The operative expression is live and let live. S, the Main Bride who wore a black tam over her wiry auburn hair, had it for a motto. 'Live and let live,' she'd say (shrugging her thin shoulders) when I made a feminist criticism of some man. You had that motto, too, my love, but your words were different. 'Everybody does what he wants,' was the way you put it. Marie thought the 'let live' in live and let live was redundant. A woman just had to concentrate on living for herself. Since she's NOT RESPONSIBLE for the other, there's no 'letting live' involved.

We were in some café last spring when she said that. Due to my depression towards the end of our reconciliation, I can't remember the place's name. But there was a poster of a German sailor leaning against a slanting tower shaped like a male member. Ha. Ha. The leaning tower of penis. His knife was drawn. In my pocket was a picture, my love, of one of your other women (the one I thought important). I drew it out to show her. But Marie shook her head. Said I was being self-indulgent. Said I should read the feminist literature of the decade. Then I'd know my love for you was only a displacement of some deeper trauma. She looked at me, her longlashed eyes reproachful, before getting up to go. Staring at her expensive clothes, yellow silk shirt, designer jeans, I thought: 'who's indulgent?' Although, I had to admit I'd just written in the black book: *Not working. Hooked on soaps. Alain came and read my Tarots, predicting a spiritual victory. Feel thoroughly defeated because things seem to be over with you, my love. This time for good. Down ray of hope, I won't be so lucky again.*

Anyway, Marie got up and walked out into the sunset. I should say she walked toward the reflection of dusk mirrored in the glass façade of the French National Bank Building. So the sun, also going down behind us, seemed to set at both ends of the street. I stood there blinded by all that light, wondering whose definition of live and let live was right. Almost missing S who was coming towards me hugging a construction fence on which it was written: I FLOW FOR YOU BLOOD OF LEBANON. What a coincidence. Now I could ask her what she means by live and let live. She's a survivor of the street who runs a little art gallery on St Dominique. Downstairs is a fish shop run by a Greek. He sits and gets drunk among his cod, wondering where all his clients have gone since his fish shop on The Main burned down. Someone torched the building for the insurance. Now he's on a little back street where nobody comes. A lot of garbage blows by his door. Dusk was falling and the weather was getting damp. S was wearing a second-hand man's coat held shut with a belt. She also had a black beret and cranberry lipstick. Gaunt as marble as befits a former addict. She often jokes about it: 'Une fille de la bourgeoisie a la nostalgie de la boue.'

We crossed over to the Artists' Café where the young men sit every day. On the bench an old woman was rubbing her stomach and pointing to her toothless mouth. S bought me a drink. After, I followed her to a bar named Cargo. The hall was huge and dark. People were dancing to a New Wave band of four beautiful women with bright hair and pink cheeks playing rock. Yet moving their hands as if they were harpists. Strange angels. 'That's junk talking,' S said. The crowd was in black so you could hardly tell the women from the men. Suddenly a dancer emerged from the mass, moving like a grasshopper. Skinny legs pointing high, one after the other toward the centre of his / her body. White sneakers rolling inward to the beat of synthesizers. Arms waving ecstatically. Around the neck a red triangle. It was love until I saw what followed. Eve. Yes, she was in black too. Rayon skirt swishing round her legs. Dimpled body swinging back and forth to the music. Hard. So the momentum brought her pretty face over her right shoulder. I could take her from behind. My hand reached out and clutched the silky crotch of her tights. In my mind.

'All the hets come here to get off on the lesbian couples,' said a friend of S's. Then the music stopped. Eve and her partner put their arms around a guy. They were all kissing. All three. So free. But there was a commotion on the other side of the room. A guy violently shoving away a girl who was trying to kiss him. She tried again, this time throwing her thinly stockinged legs around his studded belt. He threw her to the floor. She laughed as if she liked it. Oh my God she liked it. A happy battered woman. As if feminism never existed. S said: 'Don't worry, it's just a little S & M collusion.

'You have to live and let live.'

The lens turns. The street shudders. The grey woman has to step aside to avoid hundreds of demonstrating youth. 'Ici, il y a toujours des manifestations au mois d'octobre,' the Black man was told at the tourist agency. Then the agent laughed as if it were a joke.

The grey woman stands watching. In the autumn air her hair is silver, her stockings are stained. She stares up at a window above the Dépanneur Maurice. A man in a bathing suit and a beautiful bronzed chest displays himself behind a window. 'Androgyny is beautiful,' she whispers to herself. 'A hairless chest. But not hair around a breast.' She laughs hysterically. The demonstration is bearing down on her. The street darkens.

On the radio they say the earth is getting warmer. But in my heart the times are getting colder. Shhh, a revolutionary never admits discouragement. I just need to know who lied, my love, me or you? Actually, it was your silence that nearly killed me. Toward the end, you wouldn't say a word. Nights I couldn't sleep. Dawns I'd walk the streets. Coming into a parking lot I saw the construction cranes resting their long necks against a sky of pink. The department store washroom wasn't open yet. I stepped up to a telephone booth and dialed your number. (You'd moved out, but we were still priority lovers.) No answer. Meaning you'd been out all night. Immediately the sharpness in the esophagus. What if at this moment you're falling in love with someone else? Who? I dial X's phone. Her voice says hello. But I can't tell if it's pleasure-ridden or just plain sleep-sodden. I hang up. Later, in the black book, after we broke up and reconciled again, I drew a thick line signifying pain. So why did I go back if it hurt so much? Unless I needed love's euphoria.

The novel could be a form of clarification, written through to resolution. In that café on The Main, the hookers are dancing. Then the new man (you, my love) and I step into the gently twirling snowflakes. I notice your classy profile with wire rimmed glasses held by a string as you light a cigarette. After shop-lifting on Notre Dame you smile at me with your beautiful mouth, and say: 'It's chilly here, how about Morocco?' Pretending to be students, we naturally apply for a loan and go. Coming back from abroad we get heavily involved in organizing workers. Walking on The Main I'm aware of the second floor textile factory windows where women immigrants work in terrible conditions. The exemplary note is how I've learned to turn sadness into anger. The better to fight. Because sentimentality is useless to the revolution. I even keep cool when cops raid the homes of F-group leaders. Although after, hurrying under the Park Ave. underpass I hug the walls when cruisers go by, afraid they're following me. Still, with all that sense of purpose a person's really living. We hardly ever sleep. By hot autumn (ca 1975), with your affection, revolution, and even a little poetry, I'm euphoric. Especially in the evenings when we stop our work to drink.

Arm 'n arm we descend the outside stairs of our little flat. At Le Pavillon, comrades are sitting on iron chairs on a concrete sidewalk. Love-sated, I toss my magnificent red mane, and stretch my tawny hand across the table. The women in F-group are so beautiful. Rose with her small tits and Irish curls. Smiling and licking her chops as she kisses X's pockmarked face. What a sense of humour. He in turn is talking about the possibility of a general strike to a golden-haired French woman beside him. N comes in, his nose twitching as he leans his warm body towards me and whispers: 'T'es si belle ce soir, j'ai envie de te sauter dessus.'

My love it's funny you don't notice. Maybe because at that precise moment the door bursts open. And some Chilean singers come through. Playing on their high Andes flutes. A blast of Indian summer air and Italian ice cream hit my face. The Chileans in their ponchos and flowing hair are like Argentinian palominoes. Is that racist? I mean what resistance what strength to sing like that of their comrades being tortured by Pinochet. N's knee rubs against my leg. Suddenly the air is filled with the intoxication of roses. Your lit match by my right shoulder stays suspended above your pipe. I turn my head. The girl with the green eyes and a basket of flowers is leaning over the table.

Just then Comrade X takes one of my cigarettes and says: 'Chile is the vanguard of the combined and unequal Latin American revolution.' The warm blond smell of male on each side distracts my attention. Maybe the euphoria is due to sickness. You'd been so nice, bringing me plates of ice to lower my fever in the autumn heat wave. I guess that's why I don't worry about how you look at the girl with the green eyes. X is still talking to me about F-Group. Some rumour had spread that I'm a journalist. He asks if I have a high enough profile to help, through my articles, sensitizing the population to the atrocities in Chile.

In the background someone is playing a melancholic song on the radio.

'I'm no journalist,' I say. But inside a black spot rises, reminding me of the time I tried to sell an article to an editor at the Holiday Inn. Just after it went up over La Hutte Suisse. The stone and glass decor and girls in mini skirts were pure 60s. It's true we'd been flirting outrageously. Still I didn't expect him to push me down on his bed (gently). Without even drawing the orange curtains. In the shower after, I said to make myself feel better: See this as a strike against monogamy. Knowing it wasn't true, my love, because I couldn't even bring myself to tell you.

'I'm no journalist,' I say to X. 'I have a different view of history.'

The melancholy song is Autumn Leaves. *I miss you most of all, my darling, when autumn leaves start to fall.* We all laugh because that old fashioned romanticism seems so incongruous.

In the telescope the clouds hang low over the overpass to Park Ave. In the park beyond a grey woman crouches in the children's climbing box. There's a strange perfume under the dark leaves. The sun sets at both end of the streets. The grey woman stands, her filthy skirt falling about her stained legs. High above the glass tower, a little girl in a yellow raincoat. She starts to run, a sandwich-man behind her.

Things happen to them young. Those were also my thoughts yesterday watching the cute lesbians with chains in their ears and leather jackets drinking coffee in the restaurant. The elegant pussycats don't give a damn what anybody thinks. They're not tight like us because they haven't fought with men. It's strange to think that tightness became a problem, for what we hated most was rigidity of the body. No, they live on grain and welfare and just want to have fun. Still, I notice they're inhibited about public kissing.

I sit near, the better to hear. My chicita serves me coffee. Sorry Sepia, I should say the waitress. With me she used to be shy and nice. Now she hardly even smiles. Still at night I hold her smooth brown skin, her jet hair, her beautiful Brazilian lips next to mine. Not that I'm a dyke. And we dance the salsa.

Around the plastic table top the young lesbians are breathing in the smell of cappuccino. And laughing at some joke. I'd love to insinuate myself into the middle. Then I could hear to which version of 'live and let live' they ascribe. Is it yours my love where everybody does what they want as if the other weren't there? Or Marie's where a person lives for herself in order to keep from living for others as women usually do? Between the two is a subtle nuance. I think it's the latter. For they walk like cats. As if the centre ran down their backs. Yet I could feel the alienation, the way one jeaned knee trembled wildly under the table, making the spoons vibrate. Sei-i-i-. Could be chemicals. C-cocaine. Although I doubt it. Also they say the product they put on apples in St. Hyacinthe to slow their growth until they redden makes you speedy.

I get up to go. Walking carefully so as not to disturb a new vision in my head of the heroine of my novel. Inspired by them. Strong and passionate, her own person. Any pain she feels, she keeps hidden (like that young dyke's trembling knee under the café table). So that the external image with the black leather jacket, handrolled cigarette and heavy eye makeup is impeccably courageous. Unfortunately, in front of my door stands the welfare supervisor. I have to let her in.

Then today, I'm walking home again, with my novel in my head, really ready to produce. And who's standing there this time but Marie? Normally she has this gay indominitable personality. But today her sad brown eyes sweeping over my little bed sitter have dark circles under them. And in the green light of late afternoon my home looks tacky. Especially with the television blinking in the corner. I usually keep it on to make the place feel cozy. Finally she sits down, first brushing off the sofa. Don't be paranoid. She was probably only irritable due to fatigue. Because her film's in production.

I decide to act natural. I run a little bath. On the radio Janis is singing: *Trrryyy, just a lit-tle bit har-der. Baybee try try try.* Then I climb in and try to relax. The essential is to be myself. To go with my flow. Marie taught me that. Leaving F-group in I forget what year, she said it was time women started living for themselves. We were in the Bauhaus Brasserie (the comrades sent me to recruit her back).

Outside on the sidewalk the slush was thick. Tugging his beard, Comrade M had given me some tactical pointers before I went in. But seeing Marie leaning against the white tongue 'n groove wall with the fireplace burning in the corner, I couldn't believe it. She clearly had no regrets, she clearly didn't give a damn about leaving the avant-garde of the revolutionary movement. Her tam was tipped jauntily on her head over the clear brown eyes. Her beautiful mouth wore plum lipstick painted a little too high on the tip of one lip. So she seemed to be smirking as she shoved a pile of papers across the table. Some scenario she'd written for a film. About a woman poet. Said she was experimenting in new ways of expressing women's voices: 'Ce qui conte, c'est le rythme. When I write I talk out loud. J'ai décidé de m'écouter. Sometimes I even change the syntax because there's a relationship between THEIR language and THEIR laws. You can't have one without the other.'

'LEURS lois, est-ce que ça comprend celles de la gauche?' I asked sarcastically. Then, afraid she'd see my jealousy at how fast she'd produced in her new milieu of feminist artists, I said, more sympathetically, more complicitly: 'Celles de nos chers camarades mâles?' The smirk widened and we both laughed. Sepia, I almost forgot the comrades suspected me of being part of the feminist phalange. They called us *les sorcières* behind our backs. At the next table a pale guy of another persuasion sat shivering, waiting to go to the moon. That's what he said when his friend came: 'Please. I need to go to the moon.'

I added, gently (Marie angry can be really scary): 'But we women can't turn our back on everything patriarchal. I mean, take music, take technology ...'

'C'est vrai,' said Marie, 'Mais tout favorise la prééminence des fils. Ce qui nous empêche de nous inventer nous mêmes. That's why I said what I said about language. How can a woman be centred if she isn't in charge of her words?' She blew a halo of smoke from her beautiful red lips. I wanted to ask: But what if in THEIR world, I mean THE world, that feminine voice cannot be heard? Because it has some quality, some flow that's different than men's? They say an embryo suspended in strange waters gets reified, unless it can adapt. Due to its cells having a different concept of time than the surrounding solution. I read that in *Popular Scientific*. One of the American comrades used to keep copies of it in her washroom.

Anyway, running the bath, I think: if she asks I'll just say ·
I'm taking her advice. Going with the flow, the better to be myself. Still, I listen carefully through the open bathroom door. To see if she's changed her line on any of the above. For this is the 80s and there's an attempt at peace between the sexes. Also, as usual, she is looking gorgeous sitting on the sofa. A woman who, despite her politics, always loved seduction. Any man who saw her sitting there would say: a real female. The flesh is exquisite. Not to mention the satin skin, the silk undies, the soft dress. And the perfume. You could

nuzzle your nose anywhere on that body without regretting it. As if, instinctively, the outer image had adapted to everything expected of a woman. While inside there's a girder of steel. When you didn't call for a week my love, she said, her voice hard: 'Get a job, rends-toi intéressante. He'll come back. Actuellement, il a peur que tu le manges.' As rationally as a man. When one guy leaves she replaces him with another. Once I asked: 'How do you do it?' And she said: 'Je ne m'en fais pas un drame.'

Oh why doesn't she look in my direction instead of keeping her nose fixed on the grease spot over the stove? Marie, the best of me is here. But her head doesn't turn even though I keep saying to myself: Yes Marie, I'm waiting, waiting. Still, after awhile her beautiful soft red lips start to speak: 'C'est étrange, I had this dream. We were in a hotel in Halifax. You and I were pulling on a silver plate. One on each side. Il y avait une lutte terrible pour voir qui finirait par l'avoir. Finally I said: "Oké, take it. But you'll never know what to do with it. Tu vas gâcher la chance que ça représente."'

She stands up again. Her soft skirt falling around her calves. Maybe she can play the game of seduction because she takes it for exactly what it is: a game. She said to me once: 'Il a beau avoir ses airs libertaires, ton nouvel homme est très classique. Just remember that and you'll be okay.' She stands and turns on her heel. Oh oh, she's heading towards the door.

This is the city, 5 PM. That grey woman just went by my window again. In a green pall due to the moss creeping over the pane. Please froth, fall gently now on my small point. Sometimes after awhile it gets so sore I call it my dolorous reptile. Because after a certain time rigidity of the body sets in, keeping it from shimmering like it should. They say this is due to lack of concentration. Thank God, with you my love I never had that problem. Of course the focus of my pleasure was angled slightly in your direction. Then, towards the end you said I wasn't modern, there's the rub. Don't be maudlin or the punishment is getting out of this nice warm tub. A modern woman has the detachment of an artist. Never looking back, only forward. That way she can recognize human progress even if it hurts. When you took up with the girl with the green eyes, I should have been happy. I should have opened my little fist and wished you the best. I should have listened to the others who said she's good for you, slowing you down, sending you to therapy and conscious-raising groups. Helping you become the new man you always claimed you were.

But I couldn't bear the thought of losing all that beauty. On our second visit to Ingmar's we were at a kind of Tiergarten. At the tree-lined edge of the terrasse is a row of iron chairs. You'd fallen asleep. The photo shows the profile of your cheek, with wire-glasses resting on skin that tastes like the almond Easter buns they eat in Scandinavia. I'm waiting. We need to talk. The trees are twisted black and white like a Chinese etching. A flagpole goes up by the stone railing. A mast. This could be a yacht. I must have also dozed off. For suddenly you're dancing again. A woman's head against your hairless chest. Your feet in the leaves. Some striking hospital workers come up to watch. Luckily, out of respect for your mother, you don't go any farther. But how will you be later back in Canada?

I have to pull myself together. To get a fix on the heroine of my novel. Hot autumn, and despite her errors the heroine's moving euphorically towards the mysterious yet (she's certain) fully integrated third bird in that dream she had. The one with a silver-grey back sitting on a branch. Having transcended the bird in her that's dark, singing so quietly in the grass that no one hears. And also (she thinks), the dream's chattering, flighty, painted second bird.

Arriving in Montréal by Scandinavian Airlines, after her second visit to Ingmar's, she steps onto the Dorval tarmac in a yellow sweater and brown leather skirt. Over her arm a European trenchcoat. She also has a European haircut. Going by a mirror she smiles. The woman in the reflection could be out of a foreign movie. Of course, there's much more to her than that. Her goal is to maintain a certain (modern) equilibrium. To be on every front a totally avant-garde woman. Before leaving, she'd written, in the sand by the twinkling Baltic: I'LL NEVER BE JEALOUS AGAIN. And covered it with a stone. In the taxi from Dorval Airport to the city she resists stroking the blond hairs on her lover's arm. Detachment is part of the image she's working on.

Tis March 17. We get out on the corner of Ste Catherine and St Marc. In the blue air damp with spring there's a ring of chaos because a parade's about to start. I'd like you to watch it with me but you can't. You have to write a text on *Le nouveau souffle de la gauche dans les pays nordiques* for a central committee meeting tonight. For a moment you hesitate on the corner taking in the scene. Along the street small two-storey houses lean against tall buildings. Big American cars screech at stoplights. You say, once more, how macho and anarchistic North American cities are. Compared to Europe. However, you add, the mixture of races in this city makes the women truly beautiful. Fixing your eye on one whose blue-black hair and white skin may point to mixed French-Indian ancestry.

Raising my face to the sun (a smart woman knows how to deflect tension), I notice our neighbour on the upstairs balcony bringing out his hemp-plants. Down his shoulders flows his long hair. By the sides of the flower pots curve his smooth calves. I look at the full part of his crotch between his legs. Feeling languid with the spring air against my cheek. You're climbing the stairs to our turret smiling wistfully. Our room has your desk, our bed, and a bureau with some funny twisted sculptures on it left by a former tenant. (Soon we'll move to that adorable flat on Esplanade by the mountain. A sign of your commitment.)

Maybe, upstairs now, you're putting on a record by Stravinsky.

I cross the street. Yes I like it that you take time for politics. A creative woman needs space. People are arriving for the parade. Some majorettes go by. Then a bus with blackened windows so you can't see in. On the side is written ST ANNE'S PARISH GOLDEN AGE CLUB. A little English girl with her pointed nose in an icecream cone says bossily to her father: 'Now Daddy, we'll stand right here, otherwise we'll never see a thing.' I move behind a stunning woman, whose high cheekbones and blonde colouring indicate French and Irish blood. Wanting to see what makes her tick. The crowd presses my nose closer to her golden sheen of curls. A truck of Irish warblers passes. Followed by a group of men bearing swords and dressed in satin Arab garb. The air smells of people, her perfume and the earth swelling due to irrigation from spring runoff. I feel euphoric. My nose moves closer to her wall of silk. In the corner of my eye I see a Black man watching me. Maybe he's thinking: 'In this city everyone's a minority.' Maybe with my kinky curls and open trenchcoat he finds me interesting. The truth is he probably doesn't give a damn. A slight breeze shifts the sheen of her brightly coloured hair. The blue air charged with the smell of rapidly melting snow reverberates against my skin. The word EUPHORIA has grown so large across my mind I have to write. Some Irish rovers pass. Hugging the black book I head for a restaurant.

Not that place selling submarine sandwiches. I can't stand the smell. Going by, I notice a teenage girl in platform heels standing out in front. Holding a baby and saying to the kid beside her (he must be the father): 'Please carry her, I can't stand it any longer.' 'No way,' he says, taking off. 'I'm gettin' outa here.' The restaurant is full of green hats and the smell of beer. In the next booth is a woman so pissed she can't stand up. But she keeps trying as if she really needs to go. Then she gives up, falling back in her chair, and orders another scotch. 'Why Betty Hannigan,' says the new waitress coming in on shift. 'Haven't seen you in a dog's age.' 'How do I look?' asks Betty, her drunken features smiling coyly. She's wearing a brimmed hat, heeled rubber boots and checked pants. 'Oh,' says the waitress, 'you'll pass.' I write in the black book: *Euphoria: When my cup runneth over (jokingly taking a note from Betty) I sense the way to freedom. The trick is to maintain the feeling*

no matter how black the situation. I write smaller and faster,
like I did my love sitting in the Harbour Restaurant, with you
listening to the sound of ships moving up and down. There was
a cop standing at the counter. Twas earlier that spring, 1975.
And F-group was working on a little pre-Olympic anti-games
campaign based on the slogan: HOUSING, NOT STADIUMS.
Now I just have to hurry. A revolutionary has little time for
dreaming. Soon I'll close the black book and start my own political text. That's okay. Euphoria is right for noting flashes of
perception. But for real creation a person has to be neither
happy or unhappy, just floating along in the middle. The political text is on equality of women. They wanted me to do it, living as I am in such an open couple. That's everyone's impression. I order another coffee and a danish, for greater concentration. Noting that under Betty's feet there isn't yet a puddle.
Outside, the Coteau Landing Drum Corps passes.

The lens turns. In the chalet on the mountaintop they're playing an interminable waltz. A flake falls. After it goes down his
back the Black man at the mountain lookout raises his collar up.
Behind him, two pigeons are strutting on a stone railing, her
first, him after. SHE hops around and struts the other way. HE
follows. The scene repeats itself. She's really getting into it, all
that attention is so flattering. In fact this time she's going to let
him kiss her. She stops, ruffling her feathers and puckering up
her beak. And turns to face him. But there's no one there. He
has flown off in pursuit of someone else. And she's left looking
foolishly aroused. Thank God (she thinks) nobody saw.

There's going to be a storm. I love a fall of snow. In the
silence of white is the element of safety. Also, for entertain-
ment, I have the television bubbling in the corner of the room.
Watching from my tub through the open bathroom door pro-
vides a nice distance to the decadent 80s images on the screen.

On the radio Janis is singing: *freedom's just another word for nothing left to lose.*

Of course, a person doesn't necessarily understand the deep meaning of such a phrase immediately. For at the time, my love (hot autumn, ca 1975), I thought freedom must mean having you and our other lovers too. I even wrote a paper called *The Issue of Equal Access to Sexuality for Women in Non-Monogamous Heterosexual Couples.* When I finished delivering my paper to the group, Comrade X got up and said, naturally, no one denied the principle. 'Mais ce texte n'a rien à voir avec la politique. C'est plutôt hystérique.' But standing there against the black cop-proof curtains in the storefront headquarters of the revolutionary organization, I was sure certain comrades found it relevant. Including you my love, your face red though smiling approval in the autumn heat. Also, I was looking pretty good. Loose flowered blouse, well-cut jeans (bought in Europe). In the twilight my curls probably were magnificent. I answered Comrade X: 'Engels shows men have been polygamous, while expecting monogamy of women. This is oppressive. Things haven't changed as much as you think. Therefore the issue, as all issues of oppression, deserves political debate.' This seemed reasonable. I added: 'Starting with a women's caucus. Oppressed groups have the right to discuss their problems away from the oppressor.' Comrade X was furious.

Then we all went into the street. Walking beside you, I marvelled at how you seemed so much better than other men. Yes, with the warm breath of autumn blowing on our faces, everything seemed perfect. Now I could surely be a woman who maintains her equilibrium. I said to you: 'We're lucky to have the politics to back our daring choices.' You said you found me beautiful. Later making love upstairs, it was exceedingly hot. Your member rose so high, so white in the night, I repressed the evil thought you were trying too hard. But you said (noticing the glint of humour in my eyes):

'I really appreciate your new open attitude. Actually for the moment, I'm not really interested in anyone but you. As long as it's clear a person does what they want.' Squeezing my arm and turning out the light. Then we were really going to it. Unfortunately, due to a siren screaming outside the window, I couldn't focus. I couldn't relax. A voice on the sidewalk said: 'Kill the cat, the one she likes.' It sounded like the landlord with the club foot. Most of the flowers in his shop were plastic. I learned later he was getting back at Evelyn, the janitor for our building and another one on The Main. Because she would never answer the door. She'd just lay there on the blue satin bedspread with a cat nuzzling on her stomach, and call out: 'I can't go now, I'm waiting for a phone call.'

After awhile, we decided to give up. The sex having promised more than it delivered. Around the corner, Glen Miller's Restaurant was nearly empty. Feeling your discontent fill our booth, I tossed my hair and lit a cigarette. Across the table, you looked the other way. The door opened and that filthy grey woman came in. Of all things, she held a herring in her hand. We also got a whiff of October heat and dust. So painful, so euphoric. I pushed my plate aside and ordered coffee. On the jukebox they were playing a jazz version of *Autumn Leaves*. The door opened again, and in came this woman I knew from Lively.

'Why Kay, I haven't seen you in a dog's age,' I said, feigning pleasure.

You, my love, were taking in her long blonde hair and pale middle-class skin (her father's management at the mine). As she slid in beside you across the formica table. So that I got the profile of your cheek turned toward her the way you do when you're interested in a woman. Personally, except for that lecherous space between her teeth, she reminds me of a nun. She scans the menu (taking her time while the waitress shifts from one foot to the other and back again). Then says to us: 'Listen, my lover's flaked out on the water bed. But he has good dope and a great record collection.' (Her voice sounds gravelly, considering the face is supposed to be that of a pink angel's.) 'So why don't you come over?'

66

Okay, I think. Tomorrow. Tonight we have to get to bed early. In the morning we're selling F-group's paper outside the hospital. 'Tomorrow,' I say out loud.

'Oh, how about now?' chorus both she and you, my love, at the same time. Laughing as people do in incidences of complicity. If I say 'No' you'll just say: 'Okay, I'll see you later.'

So we go out into the velvet night (I, clothed in a small smile). Above us the round moon climbs cheekily across the blackened sky. My love, you're always wild when the moon is full like that. Behind us, the restaurant owner shouts: 'Get rid of that female impersonator.' He means the grey woman. The busboy pushes her out and slams the door. It's one AM. Warm leaves rush along the sidewalk. On balconies and front steps people escape the heat of their apartments. In the Hassidic neighbourhood (where we're walking) the bearded men move slowly. Wearing felt hats and silk suits despite the heat.

But you two are walking quickly, talking about a film called *Saccho and Vanzetti*. In the night light, Kay's blonde hair glimmers down her back. Following behind, I can hear her say she hated the execution scene of the two American anarchists. As she walks, her milkwhite tits are no doubt bouncing under her pink T-shirt. Under her perfect jeans her bare feet are thrust in leather sandals. At school she always had the whitest socks and panties. You listen carefully as she explains how useless and politically unfruitful the sentimentalism of the execution scene is. Whereas a good political movie should bring out the fight in people. I say nothing, being a person who cries at movies.

Funny how I remember the number on Kay's and Barry's door: 6264. And the blackness of the leaves hanging so heavy over the sidewalk that the Hebrew school with the Star of David across the street is obfuscated. Barry's on the water bed. His head leans against a crazy piece of plaster-moulded flowers on the wall. (Their all-white, old-fashioned flat is full of crazy details, typical of Montréal houses from the early century.) On the stereo Jagger is singing *Down in the graveyard ... / he never smiles / his mouth never twists / ... I know his name / he's called Mr. D / and one of these days he's comin' searchin' for me.* Barry passes us a joint. On the window the curtains flare open in the heat. I could get into this. The avant-garde red-headed woman who's ready for anything. A person just has to let go of her hangups. My eye runs up to the ceiling where plaster cherubs cavort across the roof. Kay, who's already reclining on the undulating bed, invites us to join them. No. I mean first I want to look around.

In the room off the balcony is a sofa and TV. I lay down, trying to focus on the euphoria. Everybody does what he wants. Now the Rolling Stones are playing *Angie, Angie / I love you but I have to go.* Then I must be dreaming, because I walk up to you, my love, through a crowd of dancers at some party. Elsewhere in the dream She is sitting on the verandah waiting. But when She sees you and Kay dancing cheek-to-cheek, she stands up from Her rocker and says: 'Kissing leads to intimacy.' You, my love, turn white. It's Kay who faces Her: 'You might as well know, for a long time there has been sexual tension between us.'

How long? I sit bolt upright on the sofa. All is quiet in the waterbed room. What are they doing? A progressive non-possessive woman wouldn't interfere. Yet in a flash I'm standing there. Things could be worse – your clothes are still on and Kay, in the middle, has one of her legs entwined in the leg of EACH man. Mick Jagger is singing *Time time time is on maah side.*

Humiliated as I am, I try to look natural. Turning my pretty profile with the kinky red curls to best advantage, I say: 'Uh, sorry to disturb you. But Jon, we have to talk a minute.' In the kitchen, with the back of my chair warming against against the water heater, I use anecdotes to show how Kay's mother, the boss's wife, was particularly haughty and unfeeling to miners' families back in Lively. Wearing a new mink coat to Church in the middle of a strike. Everybody hated her.

You say: 'So what does this have to do with Kay?'

I open my mouth to explain. But just then she walks into the room, followed by Barry. Soon we're all laughing and drinking coffee. In fact, I'm thinking maybe I exaggerated the whole business. Because everybody's acting as if nothing happened. That is, we three. As for you, my love, for some weeks after, your face is white and thoughtful. Of course, I'm very nice. Constantly reassuring you Kay's an exception from our general rule of non-monogamy. Given she's from Lively. Little by little, we get the contradiction covered.

At last, coming home on the bus one day, I watch the clouds bank quietly in the sky and think: 'Things are finally fine.' (Even if I'm still picking in a corner of my mind at how a woman can be progressive while defending her own interests.) The bus crosses Dorchester. Past the exotic butchers and the strip joints. On the corner of Ste. Catherine and The Main, stands a hooker eating a sundae. Waiting out a few flashes of rain. At home, my love, I find you and Barry at the kitchen table. I take off my beret and fluff my curls. A satisfied woman, no longer embarrassed by past errors. Except B says sarcastically: 'So you're a REAL COUPLE, eh? That's like money in the bank.'

Immediately I feel your restlessness.

Later in bed, I say: 'We should have told him, quality doesn't come in numbers.' You reply: 'Yeah but you can't force it either.' With my caresses you start to relax. You have skin like a woman's. No hair on your chest and soft shoulders. I also love your mouth. Soon sex will do its work, there's no need to worry. Moving from that rooming house on Bishop to this flat on Esplanade is proof of your commitment.

I butt my cigarette and cough.

Life goes on together. Breakfast, dinner, supper. 'More coffee?' I ask. Butting another cigarette. And taking up my pen to write. It's easier when we're harmonious. Your spotted eyes are watching me. I bet you're thinking: 'I told her not to smoke so much. At least it keeps her skinny. I love the way her small breasts make tiny points under that T-shirt she's wearing. With clouds floating back and forth across it like in a blue sky. And under her tight jeans, that incredible bum. Dammit, just when I start to want her, she begins to work. She's stubborn all right.

I'll put my hand on her thigh. That often gets her. Sometimes if I just absent-mindedly run my hand along her leg, she'll get into it. Now she puts down her pen for a minute. I guess she wants to show me her poem':

Sunday afternoon
with the coffee cup
between my fingers
on highway 31 the cars slide by
tri-colour birds are mating in the twilit sky
passe-moi la bouteille
sec
- - -
green shoots force through ice
sap in veins   maybe it's
unisex for me
two-one   can't
the telephone put a cross
on the road   touche pas
the lode is   heavy + ripe
with frustration

II

(I was a Poet before I was You)

The first day of spring. March 21, 1976. In the blue dusk the cross shines from the mountain over our little flat. Right now everything's okay. But earlier, I had a little trouble concentrating on my writing. I went to the park where there's a water reservoir. They just put it in, I don't know why. That crazy grey lady was leaning over the edge. In the brown reflection her tangled grey hair down to her shoulders looked like vines around her beautiful face. She's lucky. All alone like that with no worries. When my work gets disturbed by your slamming the door or hanging up the phone, I wish I were like her. I want to break out completely. What scares me is the intensity of my anger. How ready I am to blow up the edges of my existence. For nothing, really.

No doubt it's the weather. These spring nights, the air's so erotic. Also, at least once each March or April, a suicide swings from a branch in the park. Earlier I felt great walking on The Main. Wearing the pink lenses I call my glasses of objective chance. They help me do that little surrealist exercise aimed at FINDING THE STRANGENESS IN THE BANAL. Not that it's hard around here. I'm strolling along in the cool bright morning. And my eye registers a fat kid in a fur coat and fancy trousers. Very fancy, brocade almost, as if from another century. Trotting along the sidewalk beside his father who's carrying a life-size doll. Some little hockey-playing jocks stop their game to stare. An artist has to be receptive to anomalies like this. For they break through the hypnotic surface of our media-determined existence. As harbingers of the future, due to their power to change consciousness.

I walk on. My special glasses see, in the window of a photo store, a picture of a girl and a soldier holding hands under a big tree. But the soldier is X'd out and underneath is written: *Ecartez le soldat*. In the next picture the soldier is *effectivement écarté*. There's just the girl. What I like is the anti-militarism of the sequence (for there's revolt in Portugal). Also, the refusal to acknowledge the soldier's tragedy. Surrealism hates nostalgia, a key ingredient of war. (But where are you, my love, this minute? And why are you so angry?) Never mind that. I have to be prepared to take what comes. Letting each passing minute bear its fruit. A chance meeting of two lovers, as of two images in a poem, produces the greatest spark. Like André Breton who by chance met Nadja and took her as his *génie libre*. The better to see the world through the vision of her madness. Then he wrote a great novel. Except I don't like the way he used her. Oh, I'll have to test the guys in my surrealist group on the women's issue.

'Speaking of anomalies,' I say (later, as we're sitting around the table in their apartment on St Denis), 'speaking of anomalies, what if you're going along a sunny street. And suddenly from a dark alley this jewelled hand comes out. In a black glove. And pulls you in. Then it's uh rape?' Looking at me with his red-spotted face (he has some nervous disease) and round John Lennon spectacles, R says, really embarrassed: 'A person should probably know self-defence.'

I keep walking. Passing shops and delicatessens. Montreal Lyrical Linen, Schwartz's Smoked Meat. In Schwartz's window, the smoked chickens are juxtaposed on the reflection of a left-over St Patrick's float that's driving up the street. Its tattered gold paper banner reads: LET TRADITION BRIDGE THE GAP. What a collage we could make by cutting the word TRADITION and replacing it with SEDITION. Not, of course, forgetting the chickens. I breathe the spring air and smile like

74

Mme Lafargue. Why not knitting needles too? The need for emancipation of the individual spirit has only to follow its natural course. To end up mingling with the necessity of general emancipation. In this process the artist's voice at first seems a crazy song. But not for long.

I descend a hill onto a dark part of The Main. From a Tourist Rooms' courtyard steps a tiny thin man. His face is crooked, like in a crazyhouse mirror. He's wearing a children's snowsuit jacket, only bigger. I turn east and climb some cobblestone steps into an alley. Surrounded by greystone apartments and a fire station overlooking St Denis. I knock on a door. Pierre steps out of his black bedroom to let me in. On the adjoining kitchen table is a poem he's written. It has light in it, glinting off coffee spoons. And the alienation of love. Not the soap opera of the heterosexual couple, but love as in the son of a poverty-stricken Abitibi woman who tried to gas her kids. I'm envious he can write from within all this. I mean at the point where the personal joins the need for a québécois revolution. Even the view from his kitchen is pertinent. Looking as it does through bushes down onto the small cafés, *libraries rouges,* new restaurants, and the dope pushers of St Denis. At the stove Mary, Buffalo's Queen of Scots with the wild hair, is making her fifth pot of expresso coffee. The first time she saw me she poured me a cup and said (giggling): 'Better than a shot.' R's tousled beard appears from his room, named by him, Nagasaki. A new surrealist comes in, very young, his white face and black tam signifying the desired message: 'J'arrive de Paris.'

We all go out. On the sidewalk a small dark hooker with long curls twirls round and round, ecstatically. Like one of those tiny jewel-box dolls. After awhile, she comes in to our café and orders coffee. Smiling with her red lips, the red barrette holding back her thick hair as she turns her head slightly towards admirers. At our table R is tossing a coin up into a dusty ray of light. We wait as it comes down on the map of Montréal spread on the phoney marble tabletop. Pierre leans his shoulder next to mine. Sex is in the air. And coffee bubbles. And jazz music. By the fireplace are gathered some frozen coke junkies.

R's coin comes down on the map. In our game, *la cartographie du hasard*, the person goes where his coin lands. It could be anywhere in the city. Later we come back to the café with automatic poems we've written in the neighbourhood where sister chance has sent us. Voyeur that I am, I want to go east. Where the tiny restaurants and little red brick houses are as yet ungentrified. Last time, on rue de la Visitation, I saw a courtyard opening vagina-like on a middle-aged woman tottering on platform heels. Clown-farded and holding a balloon. What was she doing there? Around her, windows with lace curtains covered with little bags. *Poches à Bingo,* said the sign. Behind us in the street, the thin legs of old ladies waiting for the Church door to open under the shadow of a cross. I loved the dominance of femininity. But R said my text was full of symbols of despair. What seemed exotic to the colonizing nation was often a representation of oppression.

My surrealist coin, sign of the conflict between the power of the unconscious and our objective condition of existence, falls on the McGill Gates. Ugh, English Montréal. Reluctantly, I go over. The Waspies have just stepped from their student coves to enjoy the spring. They sit in loose jeans and humped backs under huge sweaters on the stone fence. As if their little pea heads were the only bodily part that worked. I think of the electricity in Pierre's fingers. Above the fence their long necks swing vaguely in the air. Bending now and then over the books on their knees, for exams are near.

Then this woman passes. I notice her because she's flat-chested like me. But in her case there's no hiding them. Under her wine sweater she throws her shoulders back as if she owns the street. Every part of her body wears another shade of pink. From the purple flower holding her blonde hair behind her ear. To the bright lipstick. To the winepink stockings between her tight black skirt and her lace-up high-heel boots. All of us stare in wonder as she strides by, so confidently, so beautifully. However I can't get started on the automatic writing. Feeling as I do in a situation of parasitical complicity with those thin men eyeing her from the fence beside me. Maybe the unconscious isn't innocent. I mean there seems to be some assumption of power in the choosing of anomalies. R would say: 'Then you're not going deep enough.' I do love the cutting accuracy of certain phrases surging up in our automatic games. As if reflected at us from a futuristic mirror we can't quite see, *Qu'est-ce qu'un mot d'amour? Le doute discret échangé au comptoir de nouvelles idées.* Us, my love. The love affair of the 70s. Don't be silly.

Now I don't feel like returning to the others. Pierre will ask me to go back to his room. He'll say something stupid like: 'Let's go to home and rub our minds together.' Trying to be a correct male and practise his English at the same time. Besides if I go with him, my love, I'm leaving the field open for you to do the same thing with some woman. Just when we have domestic peace again. I'll go home. Maybe you're making dinner.

I climb the stairs, sensing immediately you're not there. From behind my back, the blue-pink light of late afternoon outlining the mountain with the cross on top is reflected in the window of our door. The cool dim flat seems so empty when you're expected. No note, either, on the messy table, piled with books written by Trotsky, Marx, Lenin. Maybe you'll phone. A cold breeze from some open window (no doubt to get the smoke out) blows on me as I wander aimlessly in the narrow hall. Trying to be reasonable. Emancipated spirits must be free to come and go as they please. Except earlier today you said to me (with your usual sweet smile): 'I'm glad you've met those surrealists. It breaks your isolation as a writer. BUT don't forget your political priorities: you have a text to do for our women's intervention. After all you really fought to lead it.' This really annoyed me. I wrote in the black book: *Leninism is really like a man. The same constant pushiness.*

So then why am I waiting? The more I try not to the more obsessed I get. I know, I'll go to the mountain. Out the door. Across the park. This steep path up will open up the tightness of the lungs.... I'll climb the steps to the chalet on the top.

I believe there are 104 in all.

Only a few more now. Through some trees –

77

Damn, is that R and Mary standing over there? I forgot they were going out to hang up surrealist posters. LA BEAUTÉ SERA CONVULSIVE OU NE SERA PAS. Who's that Black guy R's talking to? Trying to persuade, I bet, that there are similarities between the québecoise and Black revolutions.

'Yeah?' says the Black guy. 'I doubt it. Listen to this. A brother was shot in the thigh by a white guy during a card game last month. He crawled bleeding to the road. They just left him there until he died. They even drove by. That never happened to a French guy.'

'Maybe,' says R. 'Where abouts down south was that?'

'Near Halifax.'

'Oh,' says R. 'You're from there?'

'I was talking about the brother,' says the tourist.

'Well,' says R, getting ready to give him one of Mary's posters. (A good revolutionary never gives up.) 'If you don't trust white revolutionaries, what about we artists?'

The Black tourist says: 'You tell me: how would you treat me in a novel? Among other things, I bet at every mention you'd state my colour.'

I step back in the trees, unable to bear another contradiction. With the gash in my stomach, my love, where you're pulling away, I start running. My feet in the sand, my head in the leaves. No, you're not pulling back. It's hysterical to over-dramatize everything like that. The surrealists say hysteria was the greatest poetic discovery of the 19th century. But they were referring to the hallucinations when a person's really sick.

I feel better, jogging purges anxiety. Helps one to focus on the exterior. This is a boot city. The boots I pass on the road are all colours. Red, brown, turquoise, green. Happiness is pleasure in the little things. Where are you my love? No, think about writing. If I were to start the novel what would be the opening? Quick, free associate. A shrimp in the labia.

Where did THAT come from?

Tomorrow I'll really start gathering material for it. Spectacles like the one we saw that shiny Sunday when you and I were walking near the chalet. That little girl passing in the stroller. And suddenly she shouts at her father: 'Daddy, daddy, there's my friend.' The father says 'yes, dear' and keeps walking. The little girl is standing up in the stroller, trying to grab her friend's hand (he's held by his mother on a leash). Too late. She falls back in incredible frustration. And others that I see through windows. The pompous fat orthodox Bishop dangling his beads in front of the laundromat run by born-agains. The sounds from the park that grey June day when I came home sick from an F-group meeting. Bessie Smith singing of painful love. As in the 30s. Reminding me of my grandmother. But the sound got drowned out by *O Canada*. Looking out the window I saw the orchestra had moustaches and their tails were draped over the backs of chairs. Must have been some sort of celebration.

Great. You're home now. You and some comrades, who say: 'We'll have to take an Olympic Vacation. The whole group. Otherwise, rumour has it, we'll be arrested.'

On that trip to Vancouver we borrow somebody's old Saab and head over the gulf to the west coast of Vancouver Island. But just as we're putting up our tiny tent (with a separate one for the little Chilean kid who's with us) a forest ranger appears and says:

'There's bears in the camp.'

'Well get them out,' I say tensely, looking up from chopping carrots at the picnic table. I can't handle it, tired as I am. Because of what you told me just as we were boarding the westbound train. If it's who I think, she's so beautiful. That shrink at McGill claims you do it for me. As I'm the type who gets bored in relationships.

Adopting a moralistic tone, the ranger answers: 'Ma'am they have as much a right to be here as you do. In fact more. It was their territory before it was ours.'

Above our heads in the giant cedars the jays scold. I notice they're bigger and more aggressive than in the east. Below the cliff in the bright blue sea, too cold to go into, the seals play. I want so much to be alone with you. Therefore, I hate to say it, but we let the little Chilean kid sleep in the small tent despite the danger. Sepia, I can't believe we took a chance like that.

In the morning I must be feeling guilty. For as I start to fry bacon over the fire, I think I see something black and hairy behind the bushes. 'Don't move,' I say to you and the kid, over my shoulder. 'There's a bear cub there. Which means the mother can't be far away.' The words are no sooner out of my mouth then a little black dog emerges. You two are laughing so hard you nearly fall down. I cross the road to the can. Feeling useless. Closing the toilet door, I notice as I sit down that the graffiti says:

CUNNILINGUS. THE BREAKFAST OF CHAMPIONS.

III. ENDING

Fluffy White Clouds Floating
Forward and Back in a Blue Sky

On the mountaintop a sinking sunray hits a tile floor. Shining through the public chalet's glass doors. The coffee machine guard has gone home. But there is a troubled rumour in the room. Suddenly the place fills up with freaks. Hippies left over from the 60s. And some striking hospital workers. Everybody's stoned. The sky is gathering like a stormy sea. On the radio, a voice says: 'Bonsoir, les amis. Nous voici déjà à dix ans de la Crise d'octobre. Par ailleurs, une tempête de neige commencera vers 20 heures.'

The tourist awakes with a start. From the chalet loudspeaker comes an interminable waltz. Across the enormous room stands the Canadian Olympic Champion Rowing Team draped in maple leaves and posing for a picture. 'Let them eat cake,' shouts a voice in the tourist's head, still partly from his dream. Now the Presidential candidate is on the radio: 'My fellow Americans. The good news is we've bombed the Russians. (This turns out to be a joke – he didn't know the microphone was on.) And now we'll have peace for our nuclear weapons have wiped the place out.' To erase the horror, the tourist clutches at his throat. Trying to think of something nice.

Puttin' on the Ritz.

He steps out into the sparse snowflakes again, a funny smile on his face.

83

Yes, tomorrow's winter. I love the solitude of white. Tonight the storm will do it, do it. Sometimes rigidity of the body precedes catharsis. That's okay. Flying high. Then appears that country road going by the gravestones and Her cameo in the sky. Just focus on something else. That passage from Colette. *Au haut du ciel, le soleil buvait la rosée, putréfiait le champignon nouveau-né, criblait de guêpes la vigne trop vieille et ses raisins chétifs, et Vinca avec Lisette rejetaient, du même mouvement, le léger Spencer de tricot....*

Shh, for a novel I have to be more rational. The heroine could be from Brecht. Emphasizing the external the better to distance from inner chaos. What was it that Dr. Schweitzer said earlier? Women often lack the moral courage to synthesize what they know. Due to fragmentation of consciousness resulting from upheaval of their roles. What does he mean? Maudit chauvin. We're not scared. Just exhausted from wanting to change the world and have love too. Anyway, a heroine can be sad, distressed, it just has to be in a social context. That way she doesn't feel sorrier for herself than for the others. We're all smarting from retreat. Two steps forward, one step back. The trick is to keep looking towards the future thus cancelling out nostalgia. Standing there among the dark oak booths in the Cracow Café was just a moment in passing time. (For a thing begun has already started to end.) The hookers were dancing, the politicos talking politics in their lumberjack shirts. Very 70s.

The place also had a slot machine, reminiscent of the 50s. They used to have one in the restaurant back in Lively. You put your quarter in and a steel hand came down to grab a present: rhinestone rings, water pistols, pink-rimmed glasses. Faute de quoi faire I stood in line with the other well-combed ducks in leather jackets waiting for my turn. Suddenly, my love, you were standing behind me. 'Cigarette?' you asked. 'Yes,' I answered, thinking 'to get through the walls of prayer.' I always thought that with the first smoke in the morning. It was my declaration of revolt. Because, Sepia, Her sickness led to Her conversion. So when She found tobacco traces in Her little beaded evening bag I'd borrowed, She stood in the night garden adding tobacco to the list of dancing, cards, fornication, and other pleasures Christians aren't allowed. I know it's silly, but that first smoke always gave a kick smack in the guilt-lined stomach. After that each transgression seemed easier.

We took to meeting at the Cracow daily. My love, you said you liked my toughness. It's too bad, then, that the paranoia poked so quickly through the surface. Starting the night they called me to the office at the wire service. And the boss said: 'I've been told you have subversive links.' I was astounded because as yet I hadn't even joined the group. After my shift, rushing in the grey dawn to the Cracow for one more cup of coffee and some sausage before I slept, I kept thinking maybe I should never see any of you again. Then what to my surprise, my love, but to find you weren't even there. Because your group had to keep moving to avoid cops at counters listening in on conversations. And word had come, without my knowing, to change to Figaro's.

The new café has a NO EXIT sign on the brick wall. (Some kind of existential joke.) I guess the fear of losing what I'd found struck pretty deeply. Because later, my love, when the comrades showed me a group photo round the juke box taken on that very morning, I immediately noticed your absence. 'Where's Jon?' I asked, my voice rising as I looked harder at the picture. You had TOLD me you were there. The comrades stared with hostile eyes. Probably thinking 'Uptight anglaise. No resistance.' Janis was singing *Bobby McGee: Freedom's just another word / for nothin' left to lose / nothin' I mean nothin' honey if it ain't free.* Turned up loud so people at other tables couldn't hear Comrade X advising new recruits. The year was 1974. He was talking of the need to be professional, to have total commitment to the group. Revolutionaries, in view of the effort required for the collective project, had to share everything. This included, euh, personal things (his pockmarked cheek twitched). He added: 'Never leave evidence for cops of *appartenance* to the group. Because they'll charge you with sedition.'

Naturally, there were certain *zones libres* (where a person could really be himself). Dans ces lieux, on vivait déjà les lendemains qui chantent. One was that funny highup apartment of the surrealists, standing on the knoll overlooking St Denis. By the spring of 75, I'm there dancing in Comrade N's arms (while you, my love sleep nonplussed in an upstairs room). I loved the image. That redheaded woman getting skinnier and skinnier from cigarettes and coffee at all those meetings. But also more intense, more knowledgeable, more daring. N and I move across the floor, ever closer, under a huge eye painted by Salvador Dali. Past those bedrooms our new surrealist friends call Hiroshima, Nagasaki. Thanks to them, our political actions are becoming pure theatre. This excites me. Soon we're going to occupy the Chilean consulate. N and I neatly sidestep a red banner on which they're painting: PINOCHET = DICTATURE = TORTURE. So huge that every letter has to dry and get rolled up before they start the next one. The idea is to shock by unfurling banners the passing bourgeois people can't avoid.

Tis a beautiful May day. Across from the cement-block consulate is a hill on which rises the phallic tower of l'Université de Montréal. On appelle ça le pénis d'Ernest Cormier. He was the architect. The mayor wants to match it with one of his own on the mountain or somewhere else. My role is peripheral but essential: that of a bourgeois woman. Pretending to be chatting, chatting in a strategic telephone booth near the consulate. (The costume is a tailored skirt, nipped-in waist, lipstick and kid gloves. Very French.)That way the phone will be free to call the occupying comrades when the cops drive up in front. Now the comrades are unfurling the giant banners listing tortures commited by Pinochet: DOIGTS COUPÉS À UN GUITARISTE DE GAUCHE. This banner bleeds down against the wall. Another, marked DES CENTAINES D'ENFANTS DISPARUS slowly folds and unfolds in the breeze. FEMMES ENCEINTES VIOLÉES EN PRISON reaches over and catches on the branch of a tree.

Oh, this is kind of fun. Outside my booth the air is perfumed with budding maple. A cute couple from the university strolls by. I smile at young love. And thank God I'm not up there with the others. I hate closed spaces, locked rooms, elevators. If I'd been in there and got arrested, the dark tight space of a paddy wagon would make me panic. That happened to a comrade who got picked up pretending to prostitute herself in support of the hookers. In the Black Maria she felt terrible, scared as she was her parents would get the wrong idea. She cried and cried. Finally an older hooker arrested at the same time said: 'Don't worry, honey, you can get used to anything after awhile.'

Still, I wondered why N gave me the outside job the way he did. His voice sounded ironic when he said: 'In your telephone booth you will be safe.' As if the English weren't as tough. We were in the revolutionary headquarters waiting for comrades to come back from postering as a propagandic preparation for the next week's action. The room was chilly and kind of dreary, due to the black cop-proof curtains. N handed me a Gauloise, his nose twitching. The sexual tension was phenomenal. I loved the scent of his long brown hair, the tan skin which in certain lights made his eyes look turquoise. On the radio, coincidentally, they were playing *Dancing with Mr. D.* He took my hand and started moving, left foot over right. I followed, breathing in his earthy odour. My love, for both of us I was about to smash monogamy. What better way to end my jealousy? Just as my head and N's moved close enough to kiss, the door opened. A group of comrades came in.

Sepia, the guilty part was that even though I did my part of the consulate job right, it didn't help. The cop cars came so fast the comrades didn't have time to organize their forces. From my little knoll I watched them getting dragged from consulate to paddy wagon. Later Denise, a beautiful bank manager's daughter from Mont Laurier, said she was held in a steel elevator between floors at Parthenais prison. And felt up by three big cops (she has beautiful full breasts) to make her talk.

Then she looked at me kind of suspiciously.

Well, I wasn't the only one who deep inside felt cowardly. A member of the central committee didn't even show. He said it was because he'd had to save his rare collection of *poissons rouges.* For the tank broke as he was moving them from a burnt-out flat on St André to another place on St Denis. The landlord burned it for the insurance. Making him, he pointed out, another victim of the greedy capitalist gentrification rampant in the city. His friend Comrade X said it was moralistic and unprofessional to think everyone must put themselves at risk. A serious organization never permits more than minor amputation, in order to remain vigorous.

For awhile after N and I hardly spoke, due to ending up in different F-group factions on account of organizational tensions arising from the occupation.

But despite the problems, the operation was deemed successful. It got good press. There was a picture of our banners in the local newspaper.

The snow starts. The tourist turns his collar up. Fallout is what it reminds him of. In the telescope the grey woman leaves the park. Headed for Ste Catherine. Display windows as in a miniscule Los Angeles. Bar-b-que chickens turn on spits. Next to a woman gyrating on a box erotically. The sign reads: EROTIC DANCERS FROM NOON ON. 'I love you,' she hears the youngest court clerk at the darkened table say. Her heart lips part: 'J'fais l'parking seulement.' His moustaches spread in a bittersweet Saturday afternoon smile. Dreaming of light shining through red lace. Of beer bottles down balcony stairs. The way it could have been.

Yes, the way it could have been. Had things turned out, my love, as I expected. With us the leather-jacketed couple, writing, working in the morning. Then devoting afternoons and evenings to the revolution. At night (after political discussions, demonstrations, union organizing), a glass of wine and stimulating conversation before we fall exhausted into one another's arms. (No one else's.) When we were still serene, I liked how you put corks on my knitting needles so the stitches wouldn't slip. Feeling safe, I almost confessed that I found Marx hyper-rational. The way he stood man OUTSIDE nature, the better to harness her.

But things seemed to meander from bad to worse. No, actually they went more in circles with variations of good and bad. It just seemed like a straight line because by last spring I'd grown so frantic (due to the failure of our reconciliation) that I thought the heroine could be like Ingrid Bergman in Jean Cocteau's play *The Human Voice*. (They had it on TV the night I moved into the Waikiki Tourist Rooms.) She's talking on the phone, to the one she loves. But nothing she says gets through. Twas April and I wrote in the black book: *Waiting for you to phone. After I saw you last weekend I fell into such a bad depression, I'm being followed medically. Can't tell you or you'll leave for sure. Ring phone ring. Makes me think of that great Cocteau-Bergman thing. But have to have energy to dig deeper. Marie says this dependency only SEEMS to be on you. Actually it's the displacement of some earlier love. Ring phone ring. Chain-smoking again. Where are my c-c-cigarettes?*

It's a good thing I didn't write the novel then.

If only Marie had come in and sat by the tub today, we could have discussed all that. I mean the way we got from there to here. Permitting me to raise the issue of how the English heroine (of a novel) might look against the background of contemporary Québec. But she, uncanny as she is, got up off my little sofa, saying, as she smoothed her white dress before opening the door of my bed-sitter: 'Même si je ne le dis pas souvent, je reste profondément indépendantiste.'

I think she said that in order to distance. In order to hurt. Forgetting that in November 15, 1976, we're all sitting in front of the TV set in an east-end flat. (Small rooms, slanted linoleum floors, swirly plaster walls.) A gathering of comrades and former group members watching the elections. When suddenly it's announced the indépendantiste Parti Québecois has won. Everybody's happy, although, of course, we'd spoiled our ballots. For revolutionaries cannot support bourgeois-nationalism in any form. A comrade looks at me, LA SEULE ANGLAISE, and says, almost worried: 'Well now how do you feel?' (Funny how I only noticed later that the girl with the green eyes watched the scene from the corner. As an Argentinian, therefore also from a country oppressed by the Anglo-American military-industrial complex, the comrades readily accepted her.) Slightly embarrassed, I stand up, raising my glass, and shout: 'Vive le Québec libre.'

As a feminist I shouldn't admit it. But my independence problems were (briefly, for 76 was a good year) on another level. Because, on the way over to the comrades' house to watch the elections, my love, you'd stopped in a men-only tavern to make a phone call. Waiting outside (twas November), I couldn't help noting you'd chosen a place to phone from that I couldn't go into. So who were you talking to that you didn't want me to hear? I stood there dripping wet, listening to some sirens go by and thinking: it serves you right if the tavern burns down with you inside. Then felt silly for being jealous again. From that moment on I would DEFINITELY change. Soon you came out, smiling sheepishly. Two nights later I'm riding by the same tavern on a bus. Going to see the surrealists. And the place is burning down for real.

What struck me at that moment was the power of black thinking.

Never mind, even a revolutionary isn't perfect. Of course she has to try. For life always goes in waves of falls and rises. Marie just happens to be going up as I am coming down. Those were my thoughts today watching her gallic profile and one set of eyelashes, slightly curled, on white skin as she turned her head a little, but not enough to put me in her line of vision. Probably trying to guard her distance, the better to avoid slipping back like I have. For her the fearful note is images from the past. She doesn't want to be a casuality of colonization. Like that stylish aunt who really wanted to be somebody. But the aunt was married to a busdriver who wouldn't go anywhere, because back then you had to be English even to be a foreman. They lived in a tiny flat. And she could only really shine at weddings, when, dancing the tango, she took up all the space by means of her gigantic hats.

I almost blurted: 'Outward trappings don't mean failure. I'm an artist.' But I'd determined not to say a word. Not unless she came in and sat on the stool by the tub covered by the lime green satin bathrobe with a few old photos in its folds. Maybe she'd even offer me a smoke. At least she'd be close enough for me to smell her perfume. We could have also chatted about the current socio-political situation. I'd say: 'What is a woman artist to do? How to create the positive feminist persona when she has internalized that the world is going to hell? To complicate matters, EVEN MEN are suffering now.' Then I'd tell her about being in that restaurant called Bagels' yesterday on The Main. And this kid comes in, full of pride in his neatly leather-patched jeans. But from the hungry look in his eyes you know he's starving. He says:

'How much for a bagel and cream cheese?'

'Two-fifty,' says the waitress, a part-time model whose picture can be seen in many windows on the street.

'Can't you just make it with a little less cheese. I only have a dollar?'

'Nope,' she answers.

Leaving, I notice he's walking fast and smiling slightly. His head high. Maybe he's going to do a robbery. That old woman next door, who never stops talking, said the junkies took everything in the last tourist room where she lived. Now she always carries her things in a bag with her. But I'm not afraid. No. No.

The snow is getting deeper. Beside my low green window a man's leaving black sled tracks on the white sidewalk. On the radio they're saying among youth the unemployment is higher than ever. Authorities fear that for the homeless, this winter will be terrible. Then they play that depression song of lust and hunger: *If you're blue / and don't know whe-re to go / go where fashion sits / puttin' on the Ritz.*

But, I have to admit, in certain non-material ways spring seems the hardest. My love, that shaft of light in the park last April. And your shiny shoulders bearing down on the soccer ball. The smell of earth with those hard green shoots pushing through. At the time, knowing our reconciliation was failing, I wrote in the black book (under the line of pain): *April, 1980. Evolution of a spring day. Trees getting ready to bud. I take my aching body to the library to start my book. Then I'm trying to locate you, my love. Wondering if you're up to something. Why am I so unprogressive and overbearing? A broken record in my head repeats the sentence: security is the lapse that makes the mouse play. What does* THAT *mean? On the second floor of the Annexe Aegidius Fauteux de la Bibliothèque Nationale, your voice on the phone says (reluctantly) I can come over. Then we're sitting in your kitchen in a dusty shaft of light. Drinking coffee from your wonderful white porcelain cups. Bent over the table, our curly heads are so beautiful, so young. A blue and white fruit bowl completes the picture. We talk quietly. But your fundamental silence makes me fear it's finished.*

Fortunately, the heroine's tough, socially progressive, external image will protect her from such sentimental weakness. But what to do then with her internal desolation? Even in Brecht you could sense the blackness. Grant it, mostly in the songs. *Oh moon of Alabama / it's time to say goodbye ... / I must have whiskey / OR I WILL DIE.* Still, I think it's better to hide it for the moment. To start by focusing on her high points, her periods of euphoria. Writing well over the top. A good place to begin would be that other spring when she's really flying. Because loved by two.

The scene is the restaurant with the blue floor. She's sitting there in a red sweater with her red curls beside her main lover. In the blue sky outside the door spring clouds are about to let through a burst of hallucinating illumination. Yes, she's with him but also waiting for N with whom she's shortly going to have a passionate affair. They've been out selling F-group's newspapers at the hospital gates. Then back at headquarters listening to a report regarding a sticky fingers operation. Ways and means of procuring new IBM typewriters from an unnamed educational institution, because the comrades figure equipment bought by taxes belongs to them as much as anyone. Why should taxes pay only for the production of official ideology?

Now, in the café with the blue floor, they have a couple of hours before the afternoon meeting to plan the evening's intervention in a Chilean solidarity meeting. He's working on a political text, but she (when she's feeling good like this) shoves duty out to think briefly of the novel she wants to write. She opens her black book diary to where she has pasted a clipping about a great Chilean revolutionary woman. A possible role model for the heroine of her story.

PINOCHET LIBÈRE RAMONA RODRIGUEZ
Santiago – Ramona Rodriguez, the companion of Pascale Puig, secretary-general of the MNR, killed Oct. 5 during a confrontation with security forces, left Santiago Saturday for London. The young woman, who was carrying a special pass from the external affairs department, boarded an Air France plane. She is eight months pregnant and was wounded during the Oct. 5 struggle. A spokesman said she was pale and had her arm in a sling. Ramona Rodriguez is the ex-wife of Miguele Allende, another leader of the MNR.

A woman with everything. Loved by two (although one's dead), not afraid to face the barricades, even when pregnant. Instead of hanging on the periphery while others get arrested. Shh, never mind that. A member of the avant-garde can't be too self-critical, given all the outside pressure. But I wonder did she feel guilty knowing she was about to leave one of those precious brilliant leaders of the struggle for another? Knowing it could cause pressures in their revolutionary group. Or if she ever feared a cop had followed her, as she walked into the grey college room where the clandestine meetings of the group were held? Maybe she'd be wearing a long blue skirt. And large earrings. Down below stretched a street toward the prison where they held political prisoners. She'd sit strategically between the two men who loved her. Or later (when they got it sorted out and she was pregnant), did she get morning sickness standing outside in the beating sun selling papers at the dusty entrance to a copper mine a long way from Santiago? Certain comrades think people with children can only be fellow travellers. Obviously that's not true. I'm going to try to be more like her. Strong. Courageous. Living every minute in the present, the better to sense the edge of change. So a day in the perfect life of a revolutionary would look like this:

5 AM. Coffee with you my love. Beside the goodsmelling cup a package. You always give me presents when you can't touch me with your penis. I mean at conjunctures in my life when I feel lower sexual interest. The quadrangle in your palm is further proof of your generosity.

6 AM. A warm day predicted. April mist rising off the park. We take the bus to l'Hôpital Ste Justine. The workers have just struck. I step off in my huge red sweater. Wild curls, rimless glasses make the guys standing round take notice. You're behind me with a hand on my shoulder. (An unusual gesture.) The Maoists, the Communists and us, all pamphleting the pickets. Ours shows how a general strike can lead to worker power. The goal is a Québec free state, socialist and independent. We also call for hospital occupation. That way the workers can supply essential services and at the same time be an example of autonomous management. It seems so obvious I can't see why they don't do it at once. I ask one, and he says (eyeing my small tits): 'C'est intéressant. Mais on se méfie un peu des communistes.'

10 AM. A meeting of the newspaper cell at headquarters. Despite the coming clouds, the weather is so fine it's hard to stay inside. We decide to leave the door slightly open. Even if the guy parked across the street is likely a cop informer. He can't hear us. He can't hear us. The debate is whether or not to

run an editorial saying comrades are being hassled by cops. Some have been raided. Others phoned. The voice always says the same thing. 'Attention ou tu vas passer tes vacances aux frais de la reine.' News like that frightens me so much I walk the streets hugging the walls. Trying to look innocent when cop cars pass. This morning I was doing just that, hugging the cement side of the Park Avenue underpass. When ahead of me on the grass I see this flasher. With one hand he's pumping his little red penis. With the other he holds to his mouth a cigarette he's desperately puffing. The smoke rises in spurts, comme à Rome, lors de la mort d'un Pape. À ses elections,' says a comrade, plutôt sec, when I tell the story to the newspaper cell.

The lens shifts again to that dome-shaped café. Inside, a group of well-dressed men and women raise their glasses and sing an 80s homage to champagne. Near them, at another table, a few demonstrators quietly fold the dove of peace. Before ordering their beer. Among them, you, my love, and the green-eyed girl. They say you behave as such a new man to her, both of you are really happy. In fact,.she's so young and beautiful (as well as feminist) that your couple has become a sort of symbol for progressives. What the new man and new woman together can do. Now that the couple seems back for good.

I was the sucker to think it ever left. I should have listened to my father that summer dusk as we drove over the bridge (our fingers covered with raspberry stains). And I, looking at the sun setting in pink and blue stripes, said: 'I want to be an artist when I grow up.' He said: 'I don't think so, you'll just get married.' 'Why,' I asked, thinking of Her sitting on the verandah, 'would anyone want that?' And he made one of his stupid cracks:

'Love insurance.'

Still, my love, sometimes I wonder if it wasn't me who lied. Pretending to be jealous like that of you. Because certain springs when I felt good, I craved the music of a trio. Example, sitting in the restaurant with the blue floor, N was on my mind. Yet, metaphorically speaking, winter had kept us warm. We'd developed our little habits the way a happy couple does. One being to come to precisely that restaurant every day because the landlord refused to heat our flat. Apart from that we loved our little flat so much. When it snowed the light was white. The lit-up cross on the mountain shone in at night. Fear in the morning was a note in the door, (as the first cigarette smoke hit my stomach) saying: *You're being evicted for cockroaches and filth.* Signed: *The landlord.* So with the old bugger I played it careful. Asking him for nothing. Having reformulated in my mind five times the way to say: 'Euh, we're chilly.' Then plugging my ears while he screamed hysterically that he was calling his lawyer and would have us evicted in five minutes. Nor would you, my love, argue with him about the heat, being under pressure as you were. Because F-group was in a crucial period of building the revolutionary organization. Shoring up against the coming period of reaction.

Besides too much domestic comfort indicated permanence.

In the mirror of the restaurant with the blue floor, I watched the comrades' faces gathered around the other tables. Sure we had internal squabbles, fear of police repression, and crazy painful love affairs. But we also had something so heady, so incredible, others could only guess at it. Like Mick Jagger in the poster on the wall (drugged look, outrageous clothes, relentless sexual charge) we lived on the fringe of a new era.

11:40 AM. N hasn't showed. Your hand's on my leg. On your face that sheepish smile that comes when you sniff illicit sex. I mean extra. Because you know something's about to happen with N and me. I think: 'Ha ha, eat your heart out. It's my turn to have some fun.' Thank God I can quickly block the cruel thought out. Although it's April, snow is falling. I feel the febrility of the waitress. In a high voice over the clatter of dishes, she's singing: 'Aider l'amour.' Rising like the sound of spoons over a waterglass. Sei-i-i-i-i. She comes out from behind her counter. Shirt tucked in at the back. But left out in the front in a moment of thoughtlessness. She is almost touching her face with her strung-out hand. Walking, her high-heeled boots barely skim the floor. We smile complicitly. Youth in revolt. Now they dull the pain with drugs. But soon they'll rise up and take back their own.

That's what we're working for.

Then Mick Jagger is singing *Dancing with Mr. D.* It's an evil song. Same initial too as D, N's live-in girlfriend. She has beautiful black hair and middle-class skin. Had a pertinent discussion with her once about what a daughter of the québécoise bourgeoisie, whose progressive nationalist family wanted her to make it for the sake of bettering the image of the nation, can do for the class struggle? Putting on my older sister role, I suggested a part-time job. Devoting the rest to politics. Because a revolutionary can't take any profession seriously as it's now practised under the capitalist system. Except maybe art. She pretended to be listening respectfully under that glowing hair and cheeks of peach. But later I dreamed that while I slept with N, she was sitting straightbacked (under her well-cut shirt the cupped breasts that moved a little when she walked) on the grass on the mountain. Smiling slightly. Not the least bit impressed or threatened.

12:15 PM. We're sinking into a jazz afternoon. Actually the tape is playing *Sister Sherry.* The beautiful waitress's voice still sings. But quieter now. So what, what angers? All's fine. You're sitting there with your hand on my knee. Still titillated because tonight N and I ... (though nobody's said a word). I notice it doesn't over-preoccupy you. You just keep writing your text defending F-group's decision to drop questions like feminism and anti-imperialism and intervene directly in the workers' movement. The anger buzzing in my mind gets stronger. Despite the fatigue that's setting in. At 6 AM we were distributing pamphlets to hospital workers. Now I'm too tired to grasp the shaft of light which was the poem I was going to write. As an artist I need to be my own woman. Not handing out pamphlets, but writing. Writing.

I have to be careful about thoughts like that. The comrades

are suspicious of any over-involvement in art. On that trip back from Vancouver, one of them said in a Regina living-room: 'You'll never be anything but a fellow traveller.'

'Why?' I asked in a small voice (my lip twitching like Hers on the verandah). Through the window I saw his *Babushka* working in the garden.

'Because you're an artist. The way you mother that little Chilean kid makes us also think you have parenting ambitions. Tandis qu'un vrai révolutionnaire appartient 100 pour cent au groupe.'

Sitting there in the blue café, I'm thinking: 'This affair will improve my revolutionary image.' When the door opens against the grey, wet sky. My nostrils fill with the smell of damp leather and the incredible provocation of spring air. N enters. You stand, my love, out of discretion. Gathering your things to move to the next table. I could never be that cool. A courteous European in plaid shirt and lumberjack boots politely picking up his papers. We beg you to stay.

We'll be three like in the Patti Smith song. *Ohhh you say you love me / I love another / you say you want me / I want your brother.* With the woman of the triangle as free as a fluffy cloud floating back and forth in the blue sky. The shadow on the ground meaning that at her highest point she'll see far enough to know who lied. For the apex probably represents the moment of creation where art is a flash of understanding in service of the future. Quickly she flips through the pages in her diary. Highlighting the allegro notes with a marker in preparation for a novel.

Oct. 15: *Something is snapping at my heels. I feel like on the edge of a precipice where you jump. If the currents are right you float. Otherwise you don't. The other choice is staying where I am and choking. Except when I try to explain this, everybody says yes but WHAT'S THE PROBLEM?*

Oct. 20: *On a slip of paper I found in La Librairie Arsenault it said: Risquer tout. C'est le temps. C'est le temps. A black priest was waiting for me outside (one of F-group's fellow travellers), the end of a striped toque wrapped around his neck. We started walking. I was trying to explain how, in order for the revolution to succeed, we had to change not only the outer system but also the inner person. For example, total equality of women on all levels including sexual. He said: 'Oui mais après la révolution cubaine, ce n'était pas le moment de parler de libération sexuelle. Le peuple n'était pas pret.' In silence we passed Arsenault's windows, a Chinese restaurant sending out the faint smell of eggroll and fried rice into the crisp air. The sun was setting on Phillips Square. Despite the cold, people were panhandling. A bag lady with swollen legs wrapped in yellow stockings. I couldn't look. I wondered if the priest thought white women revolutionaries were obsessed with sex.*

Nov. 15: Just a small entry to talk about the white light outside. I felt so good after the meeting where N squeezed my hand under the table. Then he took his girlfriend's too. I dreamed we climbed the mountain outside, a high hill pointed. And sown with trees which cast their shadows like telephone posts in diagonal rows over the green earth. Just over the top was a comfortable white house containing a couple of families. After that a path led into the woods. Transylvania. Vampire Land? Get serious. Opening our little family to new sensations can't be that dangerous. The second word association gives: 'transiting silver.'

When you awoke in our white room, my love, I whispered in your ear: 'This time, together we're crossing the bar of light.'

Jan. 13: Forty below. This room has an old beige rug and blue cushions on the floor. J'écoute Aragon, sa période surréaliste, communiste, et pense à un ancien chum. You came in and said: 'I'm going to the bar to meet my friends.' I wondered: the girl with the green eyes? Soon you were back. They weren't there. Immediately I felt better again. I won't be like this as soon as we have symmetry. I mean as soon as something happens with N.

Feb. 14: A boat sank off the Madeleine Islands this morning. Out for its last run in more ways than one. Because of pollution shell fishing has been forbidden all along the gulf. I was explaining to Comrade X the relation between industrialization

99

*and the disappearance of the puffin bird. Such a marvellous
bird. And now it's only a word. We were sitting in a snackbar
at L'Université de Montréal. Outside were sidewalks shadowed
by huge stucco walls. No windows. The university goes on like
that for a block, after which there's a miniscule patch of grass
surrounded by high-rises. 'Look,' I cried, waving my arms.
Could a puffin bird live there?' He looked at me, blinking, as if I
were crazy.*

*March 28: It's not really spring. The snow's up to my knees.
But the sun is shining madly. You can smell the freshness. You
can feel the knife in the stomach. Fanned by what's insidiously
suggested in the sound of water running off ice. Through
streets of people all stratified and stacatto. I won't let N put off
this affair any longer.*

Through the glass, the eye sees an icy wind and rain blow the
garbage down The Main. The grey woman opens the door to
Cookies' Restaurant. Its Coca Cola sign is sagging. The grey
woman walks in and sits at the counter. '... only 24,' she hears
the waitress say. 'I heard they strangled her. Lived at 24A St
Sauveur. Twas Silvano the storekeeper told me. She used to
work here. Said she was Polish. Came in the other day about
her phone bill. Her mother died and they sent it to her. No
money you know.'

The grey woman sits silently. Beside her, a man with a face
like a crazyhouse mirror says quickly: 'They threw me outa the
institute.' (The grey woman averts her head.) 'Eight years and
they got me for good behaviour. I didn't wanna go. What'll ya
give me for these shoes? Top quality. Got 'em out of a garbage
can corner of Cavendish. Good English neighbourhood. You'll
be needin' them now that winter's here.'

Behind the low green window, my tub is warm. And outside,
the safety blanket of snow (until next spring). At the clinic they
said this little depression won't last too long. Meanwhile, I'm

fine in the Waikiki Tourist Rooms, even if Marie thinks I should move. I could see it on her face this afternoon when, sitting on my sofa, she said (with her sad eyes): 'When you said the Waikiki Tourist Rooms, I thought it was a joke.' She means last spring. April, 1980. I saw her then. As I was standing on the corner after coffee with you my love in your flat on Henri Julien. Feeling kinda funny. Over my head the very early buds were trying to become green lace trim. The birds were chirping as if the future - - -. I couldn't stand to think and couldn't stand not to. Unable to grasp if you'd really said: 'Let's face it, it's over. For me the 70s spelt personal and political disaster. I want another program for the 80s.' Your voice growing authoritative. I looked up from the fragrant coffee in the white cup. Wanting to hug your warm body in the blue shirt. The calendar in the sunlight said: April 1. Waiting for you to say 'April Fools,' the silence was unbearable.

So I'm leaning that day against the stones of *la Bibliothèque Nationale* trying to focus on what's the truth, when Marie (in a beautiful crocheted scarf) wades up through a pile of pamphlets left by a recent demonstration and says: 'Bonjour, qu'est-ce que tu deviens?' Kissing me warmly on both cheeks. French people always say that. What are you becoming? And I don't know what to answer, the question is so precise.

I shake my head, almost crying: 'Rien.'

But she won't have the melodrama. She's a woman about to make it. A producer wants her film script. This very minute she's on her way to see him. She's so excited she's almost jumping up and down. When I ask if she thinks what you said is true, if you'll ever call me again, if you don't what will I do, all she says is: 'Si c'est fini, tant mieux... Peut-être commenceras-tu à vivre.' Then she's turning on her heel. My hand is reaching for her plump white arm. The older she gets the silkier it feels. I shout that my temporary address is Seville St. The Waikiki Tourist Rooms. She doesn't seem to hear. Her body undulates down the street as if she doesn't care.

It's a fact I've had a little drink. But she doesn't need to run. I'm not an alky like that aunt she loved so much. The one with the big hats who used to dance at weddings. Marie took me once to visit her. I waited on the sidewalk while she went in to see if the old woman wanted company. In the July heat-wave the huge black leaves leaned low over St Joseph Boulevard. After awhile Marie came into the lobby crying. 'Elle fut l'amour de ma vie. Si belle, la plus belle des soeurs de ma mère. Maintenant elle prend le lit avec son gin. On ne la voit plus pendant des jours.' We left. I seem to remember a Haitian mural and brass curtain rings.

Shhh, this isn't the right attitude. If I keep up like this, there's going to be a problem with the heroine. For the inside's too black and narrow. And which persona for the exterior? Not that I want to over-emphasize appearances. On the floor by the tub the olive jumpsuit is so faded you can't tell if it's old or dirty. Wearing it, I could almost get taken for Zelda Weishoff the homeless woman. Don't exaggerate. Anyway, she's always sitting in her grey rags on that cement block by The Main. Waiting for the return of her man. Actually, others say she's like that because a victim of the holocaust. The poignancy is, apparently, no one's heard her speak. Walking by her the other day, I couldn't help wondering what she does for sex.

I have to admit my mind also turned to my own slight lack. And I said: 'I'll never write a word untouched like this.' But twas only a passing moment. The heroine wouldn't have this problem, having learned a certain flair (example: the way she combs her hair or wears a sweater) by coming up to Montréal. Yes, she views the savoir-vivre as a part of her struggle against whatever she hated back in Lively. This vision of a future where everyone is beautiful buoys her determination to live each day as the perfect revolutionary. Striving constantly to combine the political with the personal.

1 PM. We're sitting in the restaurant with the blue floor. We three. Each time the door opens, the spring breeze ruffles the space between the hair on my arm and the hair on N's. Leading to incredible sexual tension. I keep writing my article just the same. On why women should join the left. In order to change the economic system, permitting them equality, not to mention

collectivization of household tasks. Even if the left doesn't directly deal with these issues now, they're all in the program for after the revolution. (It feels weird telling women to be patient. Once more.)

I hurry, because the rubby with the shopping bag sitting in that shaft of light makes me think of poetry. Maybe I could write some before, before - - - You and N drone on about moving from the periphery (student issues, the women's question) toward the centre (workers' issues) in the revolutionary movement. Under the table, my love, I put my hand on his leg. Inching it up higher, higher. Thinking about how I'd hate it if the situation were reversed. And you were doing the same thing to some woman in my presence.

2 PM. I'm so horny I can't think. I can't stand it. My hand's right on his crotch and it doesn't matter who sees. I just wish he'd get up and walk out of here now with me. I've always been like that. When I want something, especially sex, I can't wait. I have to have it now if not sooner. My love, I've been known to call you at noon at the wedding photo studio where you work part time to pay the rent. Ordering you home for 'lunch' immediately. We all think it's hilarious you work there, given our opposition to the bourgeois couple. But it's convenient because at night you can develop the pictures for F-group's paper. If the studio owner knows, he doesn't let on. He's a nice old guy.

3 PM. N and I rush along Marie-Anne. Unable to wait another minute. The street rises gently through low red houses leaning against each other towards the mountain. On top is the cross. The street opens bulb-like into the side of the cliff. Two gay men step out. Trilliums are pushing through the melting snow. N finally puts his arms around me.

4:30 PM. He's leaving my flat. I try to focus. But the air is exploding in bright flashes. So I can hardly make clear the edge of his thighs encased in his tight jeans. The euphoria is as though I've crossed the bar of light.

6 PM. You come home and I'm lying on the sofa, kind of sheepish. What a day. The sun shining on the floor. That

recurring image of N's and my body tingling until they dissolve in the dazzling air. After I wanted to play poker.

Anyway he's gone and you're here and I say: 'I've got something to tell you.' And you say, smiling a little: 'I think I can guess.' And I say: 'It's N.' And you say: 'I think I can appreciate his qualities.' Without showing any jealousy. At that moment I look up at the photo of you, my love, and me in black leather in Ingmar's courtyard. It's sitting on the table. And I want N to be in it instead. You're being so nice, I have to fight to keep from saying something mean. Like: 'It wouldn't matter what you think, wild horses couldn't drag N and I apart.'

On the mountaintop, the Canadian Olympic Rowing Team leaves the chalet. Way down below, Cookies' Restaurant back door swings open and the grey woman steps out. The courtyard is shaped like an onion. Hoarfrost forming on the fence. A buzzer rings. 'No, Tommy, I can't,' says a woman's voice from some slightly open window. 'I'm waiting for a phone call.' The grey woman leaves Cookies' and keeps walking. Leaning into the diagonal fall of snow. So damp and cold.

Then it's really dark. Never mind, I'll put this pretty soap Marie brought to my nose. A lesson in perception. People who enjoy the little things don't get lost in melodramatic considerations. They're too busy living for today, breathing it in deeply. The better not to worry about the future. In that respect I was doing great all that spring when I was loved by two. No longer the sad bird, singing sweetly but hidden in the grass. Nor its painted reflection fluttering kite-like in the world. Loved by two, I could almost sense the essence of the third bird in the dream, sitting calm and silver on the branch with its back turned to me.

Oh the sweetness of the period was overhwelming. You watched me move from room to room, admiringly, almost shyly. Or I'd come home from N's to find you sleeping heavily after drinking too much beer. Your unhappiness could be measured by the empties around the bed. I'd remember the hunger in your eyes before I left, dressed in clean jeans, clogs and a Swedish flowered shirt. With Serge, Bertrand, and the rest of the workers' commission from F-group all giving me appreciative glances. Knowing I was perfumed like that because on my way to see another man. N and I were going to listen to David Bowie records. The heavy rhythm made me sexually excited. It was nice lying on his expensive sheets. Drinking brandy in the proper glasses. Revolutionaries could have these things if they got them from their parents. I'd leave (reluctantly) when D phoned to say she was coming home. Once I said to N: 'But she's not jealous?'

'No,' he said.

'Why?'

'Because you're not possessive.'

Other times the sweetness was in the anticipation. A beautiful spring night and after a meeting we're sitting in Le Pavillon. It's full of cops so we can't talk politics. Instead (to bug them) we argue loudly how to deal with *la misère sexuelle* in this society. Comrade C (she has short fuzzy hair and a Jagger mouth) stands up and reads a poem mocking bourgeois love: *Approchez, approchez, mesdames messieurs. C'est le sexpo permanent du capitalisme. Ses ruelles sont congestionées par des spectateurs payants, nerveux, fébriles. Ils attendent. L'on examine les autres concurrents, évalue ses chances de gagner. On jette un coup d'oeil hystérique dans le coin. On s'achète un vibrateur. L'ami à côté n'est plus qu'un autre adversaire ...*

N has his hand on my knee. With the other he tries to catch a chiffon scarf waved near his cheek by D. French women know a million ways to get a man's attention. Suddenly she stands and says: 'Cest le temps de se coucher.' N kisses me and goes too. My love, you wouldn't do that for me. That's okay. That's okay. We each have our way of dealing with priority and secondary relationships.

Suddenly I'm the-so-restless. Leaving you there with the other comrades, I step out into Park Ave. Over the Greek restaurants, bakeries and the laundromat run by born-agains, the sky is black but very starred. Heading towards N's place I count 15 stray cats. Under his balcony (slightly crooked iron railings and red brick) I hear rock music coming from his window. What are they doing? Does she fuck him right after he's been with me? Without even a little twinge of acidity in the stomach? From N's neighbour's flat comes the smell of Greek cooking. N told me that one night the old Greek gave him metaxa. Then they discussed things like doing it from behind.

Walking back under the dark trees towards Esplanade-on-the park, I think a person can't always get what they want. *But if you try / sometimes you might find / you can get what you need.* As I open the door, you look up from your desk. Quickly lighting a Gauloise cigarette. Your small smile indicating you've been wondering where I was. But I don't have to tell you if I don't feel like it. Those were the rules. I wonder what you'd feel if you knew I loved N nearly as much as I loved you. Retreating from your warm hug, I wrote in the black book: *C'est très très dangereux maintenant. S'il rencontre quelqu'un et je freaque, il ne saura accéder à mes demandes de la lâcher. Heureusement je crois avoir profondément changée.*

Damn. Is that someone at the door again? Just when I'm feeling cozy. With the warm towel waiting on the radiator. I have to think, I mustn't be disturbed. For sure it's not Marie. She's pissed off because I can't receive her in the style to which she's used. Back when I struck a better profile, I'd go to her place and her friends would be waiting with good food (canard laqué, fondue chinoise, etc.) It didn't cost much because everyone brought something. But what I liked best was walking into the room. White with a long table and plants under the window. And everyone would kiss me so I really felt present. While the corks were popping and the details of dress assessed thoroughly yet subtly. Puis Hugues, par exemple, dirait: 'Es-tu d'accord avec la discussion sur l'inconscient dans le dernier Deleuze?'

Even if it was Marie I wouldn't let her in. She's too snobbish.

She doesn't understand some artists make a choice to live like this. Or if it's a bill collector for those winter boots, I could just get out and wrap myself in a blanket. Opening the door a little afar. And when the guy says: Are you Ms. G.S., I'll say: 'Sorry, she's not here.' That'll fix him. An artist can't let the noisy laws of economics distract her from the stuff of fiction. Tis late spring, 1976, and the heroine is really flying. In fact with all that energy (loved by two, as if when loved by one a woman can hardly get enough) a comrade has suggested her as editor of F-group's paper.

Except, Sepia, the problem is, the happiness never lasts. When it has reached its height, you know it's nearly over. Those were my thoughts sitting on the middle balcony later that spring. When, without warning, after feeling great, I started to feel weird. In front of me people on the mountain were celebrating la St Jean Baptiste, *Fête des Québécois*. Under the dark leaves the crowd and grass were brightly coloured. All euphoric because it was still generally believed a form of independence would be achieved.

I sat very still, trying to trace where the fear came from. True, my love, I'd been waiting for you for quite some time. But it couldn't be that, for we no longer had a dependency relationship. Maybe the people out there, with their beer cases and their tight T-shirts, were afraid, too. They just had a different way of showing it. Seeing my agitation, MY Greek neighbour and his family, whose flat opened off the second-storey balcony, offered metaxa. We all sat and watched the gathering patchwork of brightly-coloured people cover up the grass. You were probably somewhere out there among the peaked caps, brown skin, halter tops on full breasts. So what? The Greek, who always watched *la fête* from the quiet of the balcony handed me another glass. Then said kindly: 'Let him have his friends.' Embarrassed, I waved my hand and answered: 'Oh, it's not that. I'm preoccupied with something else.' To prove it, I started writing in the black book.

June 24: *I am sitting here in the style of my mother. Sober flowered skirt down below my knees. Quite thin. Darkish lipstick on my white face. A slight heel on my shoes. Very concerned with my appearance. On the hill are thousands of women in full haltertops. They look so free. I feel absurd. Last night I dreamed my house was on fire. Didn't really burn, but smoked a lot. It was in a state of ill repair anyway. You my love were having a subtle flirtation with some woman. I couldn't see her face.*

Just at that point the face of D, with its peach-brown skin, appeared on the outside stairs leading to the balcony. Followed by you, my love, and N. Under her well-cut shirt, I saw D's breast bounce gently. Sensing danger, I immediately rejected it. Solidarity is better than competition. Besides, (although she didn't show it) she was the one suffering in this situation. I mean, given the major affair between me and N. Still, my love, I couldn't help noticing how you watched her light her cigarette. And she, rising to the occasion, stood up even straighter. Which wasn't necessary. She already had the posture of a woman who as a kid was sent to ballet lessons. I loved how in profile the breast hung delicately from the perfect torso.

We climbed the inside stairs to the third-floor balcony. I didn't know why, but my face was the blush colour of the sky where the sun sets behind the billboard across the park. D said no to beer, no to coffee. I couldn't help admiring how centred she is. The way she leaned over the balcony, her black eyes narrowing in concentration as she observed the crowd. She didn't even notice N lean over and pat my bottom. Ramona Rodriguez was probably like that. Politics first. Below, a group of militant youth started shouting *le Québec aux québécois.* D's likely thinking about what the Parti Québecois will do now that it's in power. Oppose worker interests, the better to establish Québec more firmly in continental capitalism? Or lean towards the left? For some reason, between the four of us the silence grows larger, more embarrassing. We watch the throng spread over the mountain towards a huge pink bandshell at Lac aux Castors. We can't see the large mistress-of-ceremonies inside it, introducing the first singer of the evening. But from up there in the pink light we can hear her voice, magnified enormously. I turn my head. Both of you are watching D. I can feel the energy of our little quatuor shift to her from me.

'What are we waiting for?' I ask (sharply). Grabbing N's arm, I propose we go in drag. You, my love, don't notice, busy as you are admiring D's large bottom leaning against the railing. Thank God you alway say you like your women skinny. At last, with me in N's leather pants and he in my skirt, we all set out. The music is deafening. *Gens du pays c'est votre tour / de vous laisser par-ler d'amour.* D marches confidently beside you. *Mommy, mommy, what's my name / Am I French ...* sung by that red-headed nationalist singer people sometimes say I resemble. My arm touches N's in hope of some acknowledgement. But, through the crowd, I also keep one eye latched to the back of your light blue shirt. *Let it go / let it go* sings a jazz singer in my mind. *There's so much to feel and be / to live and touch right now.*

Yes, my love, you're right. Everyone does what they want. Under our feet the smell of earth. On every side the press of soaped and perfumed bodies. Tonight's the night I'll cross the bar of light and start living definitively for the present. Progressive loving means not controlling others. N and I stop for a moment by Lac aux Castors. A guy has jumped in and got glass in his feet. Now the water's turning pink. That happened to me once on St Jean Baptiste. I was on a rooftop with the high school history class from Lively to watch the parade. Except down below there were riots in the street. We had just seen the float with the little St Jean and his lamb go by. Then white cop horses were rearing and the crowd was throwing bottles at the prime minister. Somebody shouted: 'Split, the cops are coming up the fire escape.' But I'd smoked so much dope I couldn't move. For there was glass on the roof and it seemed with every step the glass would go deeper in my feet.

Anyway, N stops to pull this guy out. He takes too long. Because that's when you, my love, and D escape from my line of vision. Looking up, I know we've lost you in the crowd. Unless at that precise moment it's your shirt I see disappearing with D's large bottom in a clump of bushes. After looking around a bit, N and I go home. In our bed, my love, N and I sleep fitfully. As dawn comes over the park, I stand discreetly by the window. Expecting to see your shadow on its way home. Feet scuffling through paper and old beer bottles. Pattering heavily on the outside stairs. Opening the door. Calling: 'I'm here.' As in any domestic scene of a loving couple.

But you don't come.

Later you say it's because you were having too much fun.

Love's Eye

Late November. Unseasonably warm. I'm waiting on the balcony in the fog. Suddenly I see the street lights shut off. (Can a progressive woman sink so low?) I light the 15th cigarette. Unable to believe it. Morning again and you're not home yet. Then just as I'm thinking that your return, the thing I want most in the world, will never happen, a taxi arrives. Flicking on its overhead light as you get out. I love the way you enter a room. Filling the space with your straight back, your wide shoulders. Once I dreamed you wore silver boots. Oh God, I can smell her sex on you.

'What, still up?' you ask, furious. From the mountain all night long they've been playing that interminable waltz. I say: 'Please, before we sleep, let's walk in the park.' Trying to feel okay. After all, you're home with me. For a moment I feel free. With the wind in my eyes I can keep silent. Not say anything forbidden. Keep a lid on the strain. Discretion in love is all important. Permitting the mystery to be maintained. Until it occurs to me maybe next time you won't come home to me again. D's so beautiful. (Or is it someone else?) Deliciously round. That night of the St Jean Baptiste when already I knew you two would later disappear in the crowd, she suddenly said (proudly): 'You're so skinny. Chez nous les femmes sont faites comme les paysannes.'

We cross the park. In front of us passes the poet who loves little boys. Probably coming from a party somewhere. Yes, because at the far end of the damp velvety green grass appears Québec's most famous improvisational actress. In a pink silk pant suit. Her red hair curled over her white forehead. Two magnificent Irish setters straining on a leash beside her. Also, with his long curls blowing back from his bald crown, the actor who later incarnated Riel. You can tell they're really stoned. So crazy, so free. Ils savent prendre des risques avec le corps. I want to be like them, to hell with jealousy. Freedom is built on generosity. Leaning toward you, my lips graze your ear and whisper: 'Let's go in.' We have to be fast. We have thirty minutes before that little Chilean girl we still look after now and then rings the bell. When you penetrate it hurts. Slowly, less from passion than from habit our skins warm. The orgasm's not long in coming. Not long and not strong. 'How was it?' you ask, collapsing on my chest. 'Wonderful,' I answer, almost crying. The doorbell rings. Perfect timing.

Now, I just need to get calm enough to sleep. First, though, through half-closed eyes, I watch you pull the tight jeans over the flat stomach (and lovely bulge below). Admiring the virility of your body. How without rest it can work all day on increasing shots of coffee. Turning out little black and white images for the revolutionary newspaper. The comrades loved that sequence you did on east-end Montréal. The silhouette of a girl with huge breasts on front of the topless bar; the highway being built over smashed two storey flats; the pretty curtains of the little house next to the city dump. I wanted you make a collage of them. But you said 'The masses need linear to get the message.' Damn, that Marilù, the little brat, is pulling at the heap of blankets you left at the end of the bed, my love, when you jumped out to dress. I guess I'll get up and take her out. First wrapping her warmly due to the runny nose. The trick is to wear her out, then we can both sleep later.

Outside the air is leaden grey. We'll walk to the corner. In the shadow of the drugstore column maybe that young woman I saw before will be waiting again with her tiny daughter.

Nervously rubbing a piece of brightly-coloured cellophane between her thumb and finger. While looking constantly to the left. The newspapers blowing about her shins. Eyes rimmed in purple, slightly hennaed hair. Her white-faced kid is usually eating a bag of chips. Tensely amusing herself by fingering the pattern on a drainpipe. Knowing, the way kids do, there's no point talking to mommy until she gets her fix. There are many kinds of junkies as THERE ARE MANY KINDS OF PIMPS (sign I saw, carried by a former stripper in a feminist demonstration). My love, since you've taken up with other women, I can't get enough unless I have you every minute. But when I told this to that shrink at McGill, a real personality girl with her round dimpled face and short grey hair, she only said:
'Gail you never ask for love,
you only ask for sex.'

Times are growing colder. Maybe I should've asked Marie to close the door when she was sitting there on the nice Indian throw I put on my little sofa. But I didn't want to obstruct my view of her. For I needed to know her formula for success, I should say for feeling good. Back when I cut the profile of a winner, we were sitting on her bed. And suddenly she's in such a narcissistic trip, she forgets I'm there. Instead she's pirouetting around the room, cupping her perfect breasts under her cranberry sweater in her hand. Smiling with cranberry lips at her reflection in the mirror. I was so jealous she loved herself like that. No. I should give myself more credit. It was my acute political consciousness that made me ask: 'Is egoism required for a woman to exist?' And she said, 'Hélas, oui.' And I said: 'But what about our collective responsibilities as part of feminism and the left?' She replied:
'On ne doit rien aux hommes de la gauche. Ils ont la mentalité d'hommes courts. As for feminists, our responsibility is writing.'

But if a woman thinks only of career isn't she too male? What about the intrinsically revolutionary female qualities like love and generosity? Except if I'd asked that, she'd say on that score we've already done enough.

From my tub, I watched as her white hand with the curved nails reached for her purse lying on the sofa. Then it extracted another cigarette from its pretty case. Every movement of her arm causing, as usual, an ostentatious rattle of her silver bracelets. For a minute I thought: she's also going to smooth her hair. She didn't have to. Because she always fixes it so perfectly in the morning, there's no need to pat or run her fingers through it later. This bugs me. The way she acts as if her shell of elegance could protect her from I don't know what. Yet it's part of her essential toughness. Still, watching her sit there like *la reine d'Angleterre*, I felt like saying: 'Eh, Marie, old girl, speaking of protecting one's interests, how about giving the bathroom door a little kick before all the fuckin' heat flies out.' The better to remind her she's no lady any more than I am. Given her father was a dépanneur in St Henri. A distributor of groceries. While mine (after he quit the mine) worked in the supply room of that army bunker outside Lively dispensing ammunition.

I watched her ringed and braceleted hand put the cigarette to her mouth. She could even blow the smoke out without getting her lips all thin and puckered up. That convent she went to briefly must have given her lessons in comportment. But I needed to know, could a woman present such a perfect surface to the world, yet have a deep and perceptive mind at the same time? I was just about to decide NO when Marie astounded me by saying:

'Actuellement tu te prends pour une prolétaire. Mais tu te conduis plutôt comme *la reine d'Angleterre*.'

'Why do you say that?' I almost forgot and asked out loud.

She said: 'C'est ça que je trouve hypocrite chez la gauche anglaise. You live like bums, knowing some relative will offer you a good job when your little crise de jeunesse radicale has passed. Then you expect us québécois to do the same. Sauf que grâce à la colonisation, un québécois ou une québécoise de ma génération ne jouit pas des mêmes contacts. Donc une vie mal démarrée est vite ratée. Autrement dit, vous voulez que nous nous martyrisions. Moi, j'appelle ça ENCORE de la colonisation.'

This pissed me off. But if I pointed out to her my contacts weren't that great, she'd probably say what she'd said before:

'Ma mère me disait toujours: marie-toi avec un anglais.'

I watched (almost pleased) as her shoulders grew round from a second of discouragement. Then her eye looked nearly (but not quite) down at me. And she said: 'Je t'aime, tu sais. But I can't stand the way you're letting your melancholy ruin you.'

Sepia, that's how I blew it. Determined as I was not to speak until she took a gander in my direction, I said nothing. When I should have asked my burning question: how melancholic can a heroine be? I mean can she be modern and still lose face? Example, the way I did at that F-group women's caucus, by letting my jealousy get exposed. I'll never forget it. For I was supposed to be a leader of the women's intervention. In fact, it was I who'd pushed for us to have a separate meeting from the men (flashing my feminist credentials at everyone). The better to discuss how two women could have comradely solidarity while being rivals for the limited affection available in one man.

Twas still November. We F-group women filtered one by one into the flat of that beautiful comrade from France. And sat in a circle on her dirty rug. (Except D who handled it by not coming.) The place reeked of catpiss. At first, the atmosphere was kind of strained. Finally, a comrade opened her mouth and said: 'the problem is male possessiveness.' Then she told an anecdote to prove her lover's jealousy oppressed her. Another did the same. The comrade from France, holding a cigarette between her pretty lips, complained her boyfriend was too sexually demanding since she took a second lover. She'd had to ask him to sleep alone. I'm nodding and smiling like an idiot. But this isn't turning out like I expected. Looking around the circle, they all seem so cool, so in control. As unobtrusively as possible, I get up to go.

Outside in the dusk, the elegant grey houses around Carré St

Louis are lighting up. A couple of hookers stroll by in their knee-high boots. Another, carrying an umbrella, leans into a silver Buick and gives a wad of money to a pimp. You, my love, will be home waiting for a report. And maybe even cooking something nice for dinner. I love such quiet gestures of affection. I walk more quickly. But Natalia (she's central council) catches up. And starts doing this number on me. While I, to keep my distance, eye the ridiculous pointed breasts in the stiff bra under her turtle-neck sweater.

'Eh bien, comment as-tu trouvé la réunion?'

I know this is a trap. So as we walk along in the quiet winter night I adopt my analytical approach. Alluding to Marx and Freud, reinterpreted in the light of contemporary feminism. 'Everybody there,' I say, 'appeared to feel no pain. What were we protecting if not our bourgeois couples? As an oppressed group within the left, we women should trust each other. Instead, we hide our problems to be loyal to our men. Thus playing into the hands of Capital which seeks to divide dominated groups.'

Natalia's lip twists. 'Ouaiii, mais à ce sujet tu as déjà été inconséquante toi-même. Last summer I even saw you interrupt something very beautiful and spontaneous between Jon and D at Gérard's party.' She grins victoriously, her gums showing. 'Quelque chose de très beau, de très spontané.'

Oh God, she saw that? Yet, the party room was dark, with comrades dancing. Or sitting on the floor enjoying the warm complicity linking people of the group. For in our heads alone (we believed) stir visions of the future. Except I, feeling weird, went out and stood on Gérard's balcony, looking down at the lights on rue Mont Royal, the cheap shoe stores, the Habitant hamburger joint, a porn movie house. Knowing full well that in the next room you and D were laughing your heads off, gently touching each other's arms. That's the part that got me. The gentleness of your touches. I couldn't bear watching it. Standing on Gérard's balcony (below, the huge breast of a fluorescent dancer blinked on and off) I thought of how I'd told you, last year on the train going to Vancouver, I was against monogamy in principle. But it was politically incorrect for you to hide your lovers from me the way you sometimes did. 'Just keep it open and honest and I promise, it'll be alright,' I said.

What a fool I was.

Natalia and I leave the square and turn onto newly-renovated Prince Arthur St. Before gentrification, drunks and the left used to sit together in the back room of a restaurant there. Watching the rain drip through the roof into the soup. With obvious symbols like that, it really felt like we could change the world. Now the seams of capitalism were getting paved under terra cotta sidewalks and fancy streetlights. Never mind that, Natalia's eagle eye is watching me. What can I say? Standing on the balcony at that party, I knew, despite our principles, I had to stop you for one more night. Because I just couldn't stand things going on under my nose.

Inevitably as the bee is pulled to honey, I marched through the party crowd and put my hand on your blond muscled arm (wondering why my hand seemed possessive, when D's right there beside it, didn't). And said: 'Excuse me, but I'm not feeling well, I'd like to go home.' Your eyes have tiger spots like Dad's (it took me several years to notice the resemblance). But at that precise moment, I couldn't figure out the meaning of the expression in them. I mean I knew it and I didn't. D's head was thrown back with laughter coming out of her big mouth. Suddenly it stopped. In the air an embarrassed silence. Finally you said: 'So go, you know the way.' Maybe I'd been too halting in stating my desire. As if I didn't have the right. But I said, sinking even lower:

'It's okay, I can wait.'

All the way home you walked a block ahead.

At the bottom of the stairs to our little flat, Natalia says: 'Salut' ironically. In the kitchen, my love, you're cooking garlic pork. One of your favorites. I can't stand the way it spreads grease all over the kitchen. Also the discreet yet questioning smile on your beautiful lips is irritating. What business is the caucus of yours? What is there to say? We begin to quarrel.

Y, the Tunisian comrade who later became a lesbian, said the same thing happened at her place. He, her lover, had prepared for her 'un truc très original.' While eating it, she picked a fight with him.

Running hard, the little girl in the yellow raincoat enters the park. The near-bare trees feel like orange teeth in the falling dark. Far behind drifts a sandwichman, his boards clacking something like 'dare-to-bare, dare-to-bare.' The tourist abandons his telescope and heads downhill.

In my little tub I'm shivering. More from nerves than anything. The trick is not to get upset at past errors by giving in to melancholy. It's just that after we broke up, I couldn't face losing all the things you'd offered me. I even thought: 'God it was my one chance and I really fucked up. Why couldn't I be more accepting of who he was?'

It was a stupid thing to think. But it was that day last September after I'd seen the girl with the green eyes walking on the mountain. She had her feet in the leaves. And was wearing a Norwegian sweater with a leaf pattern probably knit by some woman in your family. Behind us was the chalet with the wooden squirrels sitting silent in the rafters. Watching her walk with her shoulders back and her feet in solid shoes I felt like gently sparring. Still, walking down the path I knew I didn't hate her. I just wanted to touch the arms of the woman who was my opposite.

Now on the radio that Dr. Schweitzer is talking about a patient called Miss Beauchamp, who due to her difficulty with synthesis of what she knew, developed a double personality. On her wild positive side, she was a distinctively aggressive person. So much herself she didn't care for rules and regulations. Then suddenly she would get dismal and change to melancholic. This stage was accompanied by an exaggerated respect for all conventions. The creep. Doesn't he know she maybe started to get like that because of all of the contradictory demands people made on her. I met this women's bookstore owner who said women often go in drag. She noticed that because the weirdest people would come in and buy the funniest books. Rich matrons who stuffed books on witchcraft in the bottom of their purses. Some old ladies cleaned out the shelves on lesbianism.

My love, I have to admit, for a long time I kind of felt split between two different sides myself. On one hand there was the positive movement of our collective, revolutionary struggle to change the world. This was a feeling of control. Then, suddenly, I would be at home waiting for you, or something, and this melancholic space would open up. Making me want to put that song by Janis on the stereo: *In this world / if you read the papers, now / you know everybody's fightin' all with each other / you got no one you can bank on even your own brother / so someone comes along / he gonna give you the love and affection / I say get it while you can.*

Yes, on certain days, especially in late autumn, all movement seemed like that of the hookers dancing in the Cracow Café on The Main. I mean going in two opposite diretions at the same time: first left foot over right; then turning and doing exactly the reverse, right over left. Maybe that explains our disastrous reconciliation last winter. For first we'd broken up and I was flying high, going to New York on a train along the Hudson River with Marie. Outside the wide flat river between its lush muddy banks reminded me of Huckleberry Finn. Coming back into Montréal's Gare Centrale in my New York raincoat, the sun was shining. It was autumn. And though I didn't know it yet, underneath a hidden hunger was leading directly to the line of pain. This was recorded in the black book: *Oh God, we're back together again. And I think you want youth, naivety in me. Because when I project it you feel better. Since I can't be both naive and the strong woman I was becoming at the same time, I have to fold myself up smaller and smaller. For us to get along.*

Marie was furious when she came into my room just after that and found me reclining pale and tired against the pillows on the rug. She said:'Tu m'inquiètes. If you can't handle his polygamy, drop the whole thing.' I didn't tell her that choice should have been made four years earlier. I mean on that beautiful July morning back in 1976. When we were about to board the westbound train for our Olympic Vacation. And you confessed to me you had another lover (you wouldn't say who). All the way to Vancouver, I waver between two contradictory aims:

1. To ignore it and write poetry in this gap of summer air between the endless grime of heavy struggle against the deathly laws of capital.

2. To get you to stop.

But what hurts most of all is being in the space between the two. In the interest of figuring it out I buy a black book and inaugurate a diary:

Montréal-Toronto: Pulling out of la Gare Centrale. Must quickly get out of this space of fear and anxiety I just fell into. Can't afford to spoil even one beautiful day like this. If I go on acting such a possessive ass, I'll end up like a wrinkled prune. So tight. These old conventional love patterns have to be unlearned. Somebody help me fight.

Now I'm not sorry I gave you a little infection while making love. The seed, planted by me innocently enough, just grew and grew. Ha, your prick is blossoming so, you won't be able to make love with anyone. Shhh. Toronto Stopover: Graffiti near Union Station: IN TORONTO THERE ARE NO CLASSES. JUST THE MASSEYS AND THE MASSES. Then a theatre marquis: No Sex Please. We're British. A Hilariously Funny Play. Toronto-Winnipeg: Perhaps your difficulty with emotional self-expression will be improved through these other encounters. And what you gain from it will be fed back into our relationship. So there, I should go along with it. Unless this is all part of the dynamic of the dissolution of our love?

I'm so anxious. This train seems to be going nowhere fast. Yet nobody complains about the two hour delay in Kapuskasing. No voices of protest against the freezing air-conditioning.When they turn it off the heat pours out. Outside it's sun-sparked birch leaves, flower boxes on the little stations.

At midnight a guy opens a novel across the aisle. Four hours later he's advanced about four pages due to the wild party around him. He looks up and smiles wryly at the partyers every once in awhile.

On the radio, Johnny Cash is singing I walk the line. *Back when love was the only answer things were easier. I keep putting off writing because, because*

Winnipeg Stopover: Calm for the first time since the 'news'. Feeling in love today. Ready to embark plus à fond on the great poetic adventure, i.e. living the contradiction between (the need for) love and freedom. The solution as a comrade says here (I think he's a virgin) is not to be burdened. Reading the Russian futurists, about Mayakovsky in his yellow shirt. Out by the lake where we went there were some yellowheaded blackbirds, such as we never see back east. West from Winnipeg: Johnny Cash still on the tape in the bar car. Some québécois came in wearing T-shirts that said: I've been in jail. *They're on their way to pick fruit in the Okanagan Valley. Yesterday while sipping beer, a cowboy showed me a pornographic snapshot with a ruby crotch on it. Then he talked about the devil. A little girl from the east, hiding behind a seat, said she'd never heard of the devil.*

There was a thunderstorm, bright in the night. Lighting the black prairie after the fantastic twilight. Heather hues of purple, white, mustard yellow. The rivers wound round and round. Like snakes. I was hoping the thunder would wake you up. So we could talk about how to combine my wellbeing with your new relationship. 'Sweetheart,' I'd say, gently stroking your smooth arm. 'We have to talk.' This made you sleep even harder.

Sometimes I get so unhappy I can't talk anymore. Then I think I'm going neurotic. Then I talk and my throat hurts with the words coming out. Or you get upset. I feel like I'm speaking another language.

This trip is like a long dark tunnel. When we get to Vancouver, I'll see, maybe, how to be free.

But this is the city, 1980. A heroine can't just be sitting on some train writing in a diary. It isn't modern. As a setting, my little television-lit room is better. On the table sits a package wrapped in red-and-white polka dots nostalgic of the 50s. Marie must have left it. I can't deny I like her savoir-vivre. Once in her house (I was taking in her glowing pine table, the perfect cream walls, the brandy-coloured cut-glass decanter, and other turn-of-the-century décor popular in the 70s), I blurted out: 'Why must you surround yourself with so much beauty?' She answered: 'Pour me distraire du mal.' Sepia, at that moment I saw for the first time the terrible sadness in her eyes. And felt I was beginning to know what modern was.

Now people are using little 50s objects of nostalgia to dull the pain. Take those kids running the restaurant called Bagels' on The Main. They have 50s suits, lime-green 50s formica table tops, 50s music, 50s shoes. Yet you can tell by the way they move they keep a distance from the old 50's melodramatic values. All their world's a stage on which they're cool ironic players. Maybe a nice touch would be to have the 80s heroine walking into their nostalgic 50s restaurant:

The heroine, une anglaise haïe par l'Histoire (for social context), mais aimée par quelques amies, opens the door. On the black glass in white letters is written:

BAGELS'

UN DINER [DA-Y-NÈRE] – (the French way to pronounce the English word, in concession to the law which says signs shall be in French only).

OUVERT 24 HEURES

She sits down at a green table. The clear oval glass of the window has a red neon. The theme is movement. In the air a bubbly jazz song. A flock of pigeons make a low circular swoop over the square outside. Under a bright blue sky the leaves are blowing. A Jehovah's Witness family holds up their booklets beside the iron fence. Older male, kind of fat. Attractive younger wife in tailored skirt. In the beginning the little girl (all dressed in red) is really enthusiastic. All kinds of people pass: a punk with white hair, a sad-looking fat lady, a guy dragging his bare foot behind him on the sidewalk. But nobody looks at the red, green and orange-covered books they're holding up. The little girl glances at her Mommy and her Daddy. Wanting to tell them what she's noticed. At the same time wanting to be obedient.

The heroine's observations are distracted by a draft. The restaurant door has opened, letting in a woman with reddish hair almost the colour of her own. She's dressed in a longish skirt and wearing laced rubber boots. What's weird is she is carefully carrying (as if it held a bird) a bird cage with nothing in it. She says to the waitress:

'I'm on welfare, I want a coffee. I'll pay you next week.'

'Sorry,' says the waitress, 'we don't do that here.'

The redhead's furious. 'What's wrong?' she says, her voice rising. 'You jealous?' Then to the empty cage: 'Come on, we're leaving.'

The heroine trembles a little as she raises her coffee to her lips. Thinking she senses how a woman can end up like that. By being a slave to love until she hates herself. Through the coupole in the painted glass above her table, she sees the woman with the cage disappear down the street. In the background Bessie Smith is singing: *Nobody cares for me.* The heroine likes the paradox: that in singing those words Bessie Smith made herself loved by everyone. As if the poetry in her could help a melancholic woman move forward through the present. Oh my love, on the trip to Mont Laurier, I clearly saw that option. I mean a woman just has to walk that tense line between the sadness (past) and the beauty (future), the better to live now. But some fiend in me made me do the opposite.

Twas the late 70s and snowing hard. Already you could feel the bottomlessness of the 80s. Coming out of the Métro I see this kid running away from home. For some crazy reason I want to go with him. He's hardly visible in the thick flakes. Still he has a hockey mask completely over his face. So tiny there with his light knapsack on his heavy snowsuit. Where is he going, already so far into the city?

Instead I head home. Worn out, I guess, from the endless

stress of holding onto you (while quietly writing from another angle in the black book): *These boring years of ups and downs with you may seem useless. But they must give something for my writing. Like this odd feeling once in while that it has really been* you *(past) who's cared and I who wanted out. Yet loaded with guilt I always take a defeatist attitude. And end up feeling I'm the rejected one.*

But will I find you there? Earlier, waiting for you at the cathedral, I was afraid you were with D. To be exact, it was outside L'Église St Henri. I'd been waiting for awhile. Thinking how as a kid I kind of looked like the redcheeked girl on the Coca Cola sign some rebel had tacked on the church's wall. When you didn't come, I took my feet wet with November slush into the church and burned a candle for us. You'd have killed me if you knew. Then I saw you walking over the pink snow. An old FLQ manual under your arm. Your baggy pants were blowing in the wind.

How I laughed. You hadn't been with D at all. Instead you'd been browsing through a second-hand bookshop. The manual you bought was a collector's item from the 60s. Full of amateur directions for urban terrorism. *Comment faire une bombe. Tu prends du fil. Ça coute dix cents, la valeur d'un anglais.* We repeated to each other that sentiments like that will be normal as long as there are dominating and dominated people. From the slums of St Henri (mostly French) we raised our heads to look at the mansions climbing up Westmount Mountain (mostly English). Between the two, separating the oppressed from the oppressors, a huge chasm that the Canadian Pacific Railway trains run through. Some ragged old woman stood down there watching. I said excitedly, leaning forward from the waist, and stretching my hand in a stagelike gesture:

'And there you have the history of Canada in a nutshell.'

You said you liked me best when I said intelligent, interesting things like that.

We drew closer in the falling snow. Chibougamou came out of his tavern. I had on my big hat. Under, tightly tucked, the orange curls. We stopped to look in an antique window at an old painting called *Veronica washing the face of Jesus*. We turned onto St Henri square. Past some painted gates held closed with rope. The sky was leaden over the houses with their little belfries. You pointed to one in which you said the organization printing press was temporarily located. The door opened and out stepped the girl with the green eyes. For the first time I noticed the dimple in her chin. The two of you gazed at each other lengthily. But rumour had it she'd become a dyke. On the next corner you said mysteriously: 'See you later, I have to run a little errand.'

This pissed me off.

On the Métro all the way up narrow Marie-Anne, with its flat roofs rising slowly toward the mountain cross, I wonder where you are now. Oh Mama, why'd you put this hole in me? In the thick flakes, I turn the corner. And there, to my surprise, my love, your sweet grin is waiting in the window of a rented car outside our house.

'Come on, we're taking a little trip.'

I climb in.

The road to Mont Laurier goes over mountains and through forests. It leads in the dark to a log motel with moose antlers over the door. I'm the-quite-happy (although in the corner of my mind lurks the shadow of the other). In our room, you take me in your arms, saying:

'We needed this.'

Tis only after sex on the orange bedspread that I ask sweetly (putting my hand on your arm and sounding – almost shy): 'Does this mean uh with you and D it's finished?' Silence. 'I mean you told me awhile back you're mostly friends, with only a little sex now and then....' Silence. 'Is that still true?' Oh what a mistake I've made. I can feel your tension rising. Finally you answer: 'In a relationship, as we decided long ago in Morocco: everybody does what he wants.'

Rashly, I pursue it: 'But what does she mean to you?'

You (now your temper's boiling): 'I don't know.'

This really scares me. I was hoping for 'not much' or something neutral. Desperately I look around the room. Varnished log walls, a pale knotty-pine dresser, and a mirror surrounded by the same material. I've got to get control. Now that I've made you furious. And I, I'm upset because whenever we're together she's there too whether or not she's mentioned. If I fuck this weekend up she'll win points. Besides a free woman isn't jealous or possessive. Stroking your lovely hair (it still has a blond Northern European light in it) I say: 'Sorry, we must both be overtired' and leaving you, go downstairs.

The empty lounge is decorated with stuffed birds. I push a table near the fireplace. Feeling terrible although a resentful corner of my mind says it's okay to insist on reassurance. No, no that's not the way to win. Behind my head the stuffed eagle, some owl that's almost extinct now, and a pretty blue little warbler watch. I just have to *Let it go, let it go,* as the jazz song says. But what if you love her more than you love me? With her jetblack hair and her breasts so white. In the dream, my love, she was floating through the room naked on her stomach and you floated right out after her. When I told it to the shrink at McGill, she said:

'Ha ha Gail, she's really the temptress, isn't she?'

The little warbler has tiny eyes, so bright, yet painful. Why do I spontaneously identify with (her?).

The grey woman sloshes through a piss puddle and climbs some stairs. In the park the little girl crouches in the children's climbing box. Panting heavily. Her warm crotch touches the cold ground. Among the branches the sandwichman flutters like a lost bird.

From my little tub now I can smell the incredible aroma of coffee. I'll drink some soon because my widow's beak's about to quiver. Then I can get out. Oh yes white froth it's coming coming—please stay warm as a sperm river. On the radio Janis is singing: *I'm gonna show ya baybee / that a woman can be tough / so comeon now / take a little piece of my heart...* Not too feminist, due to the era. But you could tell, by the way she moved on stage, she was coming on to women too.

Except yesterday I became afraid feminism as an issue was being superceded by hunger again. The scene was across from a café on The Main where I was drinking my second cup of good expresso. The door of a little flat opened and they threw a tenant out. He had two bags, recent sneakers and a thin but neat blue nylon jacket. High Indian-looking cheekbones like my brother. In the face I recognized the tension of a man who no matter what he did would never make it. Standing on the step he doused a cigarette. Carefully against the wall before he put the other half of the butt back in his pocket. Then picking up his bags he walked south.

Maybe he's a tragic personality. Marie tried to put me in that slot once. Twas the late 70s (not long after Mont Laurier) and we, my love, had just decided to live apart, the better to be ourselves. If anybody asked, we had an answer: PRIORITY LOVERS BUT WITH SEPARATE RESIDENCES. Anyway Marie came into my flat on Esplanade. I'm sitting on the white rug, knees sideways, very thin in a pale blue sweater and tight jeans. With a blue band around my forehead holding my wild orange curls. And she says: 'Mon Dieu, tu es belle quand tu es triste.'

I have to admit I found that kind of weird. To look so cool when I was behaving so unmodern. For, glad as I was to see you move (due to the terrible accumulation of fatigue from waiting up at night), the quietness of my empty room was disconcerting. Sometimes I'd do this shameful seduction dance when you dropped in. Letting my pink 40s-style satin bathrobe slide off one shoulder until you couldn't resist. You loved the line leading from my shoulder to my neck. On those particular nights, we had a lot of sex. Or else I'd do the opposite and pick a fight. *A very tense evening* (I wrote in the black book). *Partly I brought up a lot of shit after discovering there were more in your life than D. You were going on about how important the girl with the green eyes was to you, how it's a friendly but very physical relationship. Blah, blah.*

Sepia, the truth is I'd sunk so low that at the precise moment

Marie came in, I was in the act of throwing the *I Ching*. So obsessed I couldn't bring myself to stop and kiss and hug her (although anticipating the sweetness of her presence) until I'd read *I Ching*'s answer: *You are powerless and powerful. Deep down, friend may love you more than you love him. But he is currently a spoiler.*

We took our coats and went out. Walking beside her in the January snow I suddenly feel better. Even calm, content. The big flakes falling almost veil the lit-up triplexes along the sidewalk. And in the cold air, as we move close, I catch a whiff of the impeccable grooming under her red cloth coat. Why, despite the cold, she's probably wearing perfume high on her thighs this very minute. Oh the beauty of Québec. Of course, due to its semi-colonial infrastructure, the pollution is abominable. I was thinking of writing a children's book about a small bird that lost its song on account of the air quality. What I missed, my love, in periods when you and I saw each other less, was being able to share my little projects immediately, spontaneously with you. This very morning when I saw the large sticky snowflakes adhering to the dirty pane, I wanted to phone you about my idea. Knowing you'd be impressed by the direct message in it. But what if you weren't alone?

We turn onto Park Ave. Through the swirling snow I can see an owl on an upper sill of the meeting hall where we are headed. The strange note is, it's been there since that Trotskyist War Measures Act meeting in 1970 into which I accidentally stumbled. I remember the speaker behind the table saying: 'This Act proves that when you scratch the surface of bourgeois democracy, you get totalitarianism' just as I sat down. Then something made me look toward the window. And there was this owl sitting there with strangely stiff feathers. The speaker paused and said: 'Camarades, I'd like you to welcome the member of la Gendarmerie Royale who just joined us.' Sure enough, a guy with the only short hair and pressed shirt in the place was sitting down. Everybody turned and jeered. After, in the bar, a famous félquiste recently out of jail sat next to me. He had a beautiful fur hat and clear blue eyes. Later they found him murdered (mysteriously) in Paris. On the way home that night I noticed the owl was still up there on the snowy sill.

Marie and I enter a restaurant for takeout cappuccino. At least I do. She says: 'Non merci, j'ai déjà pris mon café.' I can't see what difference that makes. I mean two coffees never killed anybody. While the Spanish waiter whips the white foam over the fragrant steaming cup, she leans against the bar and watches me carefully.

We cross the street and climb the stairs to the meeting room. Opening the door, a disturbing mixture of perfume, fur and wet leather fill our nostrils. The place is now a feminist drop-in centre, all carpeted and cushioned. I sit on the floor, leaning against the knees of a large lesbian who's sitting on a sofa. She immediately begins to stroke my hair. The subject is *La créativité des femmes: rapport entre le corps, le quotidien, le langage.* I love their openness. A woman called Louise gets up and says even among her hetersosexual friends, many have temporarily given up relationships with men. I prick up my ears. Feeling there is something very avant-garde about this statement. Also, says Louise, pushing back her permed blonde Afro hair, some feel we women should even take total power over children (denying their paternity), the better to create a truly subversive community. One thing was sure: to maintain solidarity among themselves, the sisters in her particular group refused to abet male power by sleeping with the lovers of each other.

Sepia, I like that so much I almost get up and cheer. Except the lesbian who has her hands on my head is shouting mockingly:

'T'en es juste arrivée là. Ce sont des choses que nous autres lesbiennes savons depuis toujours.'

I'm trying to adjust my mind to this even more radical-feminist line, when a woman with black curls and highheeled boots says, a little timidly, that she really likes men, especially sex with them. It's extremely rare for her that penetration feels like aggression (as the other sisters claim).

'Too bad for you,' another lesbian shouts. 'Now when are we going to talk about our relationship to language?'

Leaning forward, very excited, I say women must have a different relationship to language BECAUSE OUR LIVES ARE DIFFERENT. Somebody says Virginia Woolf wrote almost the same thing decades ago. But my words keep tumbling out. I say maybe we feel resentment towards men because there's deference to the male in all sectors of society, including the left (a few boos). But this obvious exclusion at least points to the possibility we have another place to speak from (I got this from a book Marie lent me). And understanding this might even alter syntax. But it's a collective process that will take utter concentration, hence the necessity of solidarity around issues like monogamy.

Marie's head is cocked, listening carefully. After in the quiet street (the snow has stopped), she says my speech was 'très beau bien que pas spécialement nouveau'. We keep walking in the damp silence of Park Ave. My euphoria is phenomenal. I take her arm and lean my head upon her shoulder. Feeling like a new person. She opens her pretty mouth, about, I think, to praise again.

'Gail,' she says. 'Tu ne prendras pas en mal ce que je vais te dire?'

'What?'

'J'ai compris ce soir qu'est-ce qui est tragique dans la vie d'une femme. Je l'ai compris, car je l'ai vu très clairement chez toi.'

'What?' (as nonchalantly as possible).

'C'est que tu ne sembles pas pouvoir faire coincider du tout qu'est ce que tu vois comme vie possible avec qu'est-ce que tu es, qu'est-ce que tu vis actuellement. You almost said it earlier: it's as if the words or maybe even the syntax have to be invented to close the space between what you're living now and future possibilities. Your life is an illustration of this problem. Yes, with you it's very obvious, very painful.'

She has no business putting me down like that. I tell her I disagree with her use of 'tragic'. That in modern times, tragedy has gone beyond the level of the individual to the human race. Why now it's proven that the American administration wants limited nuclear war, not peace.

'Precisely,' says Marie. 'The Americans are caught in their own monologue. So they can't see the way forward. Something we women have to be careful to avoid.'

Yeah, well, I learned long ago how to deal with that. To see the way out of any situation, a person just keeps checking her performance from all the angles. So she doesn't make the mistake of that kid in 1960 who wanted to win the SAVE OUR FORESTS poster contest. The kid worked all day, coming up with a great slogan. Then using the words to make a beautiful design in the allotted space. Carefully measuring the spaces between every letter she'd created. Colouring it so nicely with a little illustration on the bottom. Stopping only once when they came to take the school photos. But at four o'clock the teacher stood by the kid's desk, looking down, and said: 'It's very nice but you'll have to rip it up.' 'Why?' asked the kid, tears flooding into her soft brown eyes. 'Because your BUT YOUR BUTS doesn't mean a thing. The butt you mean is spelled with a double T.' Walking home in the snow past cans on the maple trees to catch the dripping sap, the kid wondered if some essential fault in her had made her take beautiful care of certain details while forgetting the essential.

Her father hated the school picture. Couldn't stand the way she's biting her lower lip.

The tourist turns onto The Main. It's 6:30 PM. Through the slant of snow falling he sees the abandoned doll Babe Ruth in front of the sausage shop. Of course he doesn't know it belongs to Anthony Surtado whose father said: 'What are you? Some kind of fag with his prick tied back? Get rid of that doll.' On the frozen ground of the children's climbing box lies a yellow raincoat. The little girl (Anthony's friend) runs through the dark. At each breath her heart leaps painfully into her mouth.

The tourist keeps walking. Chibougamou comes out of yet another tavern. His pants are wet. In the theatre version they put a balloonful of water under his belt. However, the actor decided he wanted to really pee in public to see how it felt. As the hot pee hit the stage he nearly fainted. Because of course he couldn't stop it. Surrounded by horrified mouths (they seemed horrified but maybe they didn't even really notice) he felt as if time had locked.

A heroine locked in time could be the ruination of a novel. I should get out and write this down. Still, sitting in Bagels', the heroine seems to think of time as moving more like in music than in a storyline. For she always wakes up with his perfect body glowing like the silver of illusion in a corner of her mind. While in another corner glows the free woman faintly outlined in the future. Even while still with him (therefore lacking distance) she wrote of this contradictory sonatina in her diary: *Winter. Return of light (snow) and inspiration. And the sad-sweet combination of you and I in bed. Warmth, then battle. What is this revolt in me that must destroy (half-baked) love?* The question is, if she's fractured over time with the inner self shining bright and dark like that, from what angle can a person start the story?

Maybe I could do like those kids down in Bagels', pretending the angle is back in the 50s. One of them wears a dress (she also has bobbed hennaed hair) like Mother used to wear. I saw it in a picture. She is standing in the shadow of the station. The wool dress is dark green with some kind of gold studs across the chest. Her high cheekbones tinted pink. And a wonderful gold light shining out of her dark brown eyes. She's leaning against our future father who's in a dark uniform. The uncle who showed it to me on the trip to Vancouver said:

'After marriage, she became a real bitch.' I stared back into his fat born-again face and retorted:

'Actually, She wanted to go to Africa.'

Then he said I killed her with my wildness.

But Sepia, I know that isn't true. For certain nights She came to me when I needed her. Once (I know this sounds weird) I even prayed to her and she answered in a dream. It was after that women's meeting when I was feeling first euphoric, then kind of plunging down. And Marie wouldn't come up (to the empty flat) for a drink or something. Because she had to work next day. So on Park Ave., I kissed her goodnight (offhandedly) and went home. Crawling into bed, I could really sense the darkness of the kitchen. To focus on something else, I opened the black book at the part marked: *Trip back from Vancouver, 1976: Heading east over the dry gulches of Moose Jaw, I know I have to make a choice. But through Regina (where comrades said the native ghettos would one day blow like Harlem or Detroit), then through Winnipeg and the forests of Ontario, I still can't decide to say: 'Okay, my love, I accept your non-monogamy,' or, 'I'm sorry but we're through.'*

After which, I was thankful to fall asleep. Then the birdsweet voice of that lesbian in her telephone booth starts singing: 'There are two tongues in every language.' Laughing her head off. Everything is fine but is it the real telephone ringing? A wrong number or an obscene phone call? And getting back into bed is that a real mouse I see on the floor? Soon they are on the bed and on the sheets, tickling me. Back in Lively the farmers put their bed legs in pails of water to keep them off. But I can't do that since my mattress is on the floor. I answer the ringing phone again and Her cameo says I'm paying for unfaithfulness to my young officer. My love that is too much. I show Her my eye which is turning black and blue. And the blood vessels bursting round my cheeks. There was a moment of silence. Then Her cameo concedes:

'Okay, I see what you mean.'

I awake at dawn with a terrific feeling of déjà vu. Making me laugh because of how it puts everything in context. Outside the street is glistening with sun and piled with new snow. I'll give you one more chance to talk my love. With a new man like you I'm sure it's possible. Although sometimes our conversations get confusing. Example, if I'm feeling weak and scared while you, sitting on the edge of my desk, are saying my personality's too strong and overbearing. Maybe a special diet will help to clear things up. A woman's magazine says excessive bile may be cured by no sugar, no coffee, no cream, no eggs, no meat. And I forget what else to clean the system out.

I decide to go out. Walking down the winding stairs, I breathe the white air of the park, deeply. Enjoying the gargoyles on the housetops looking down at me. And the crunch of feet on the thick, protective carpet of snow. I'm headed towards the Golden Palace Grill. Forgetting to think consciously that you, my love, are sometimes there. (My policy being to avoid you mornings now you've moved, because God knows what bed you're coming from.)

Yes, you're there. In the end booth, drawing a list of target restaurants for union organizing. I sit down, hoping you won't see my black circles. Maybe the pinkish light shining through the red fishnet curtains will soften them. Making us glow as if we were in some corny religious painting. But your green eyes with the tiger spots scrutinize me carefully. A small smile grows on the beautiful mouth, as if you're seeing me for the first time and kind of like it.

I smile back, feeling warmer. And say (the diet's for later): 'Some coffee would be nice.' In the next booth a fat old woman is telling her companion: 'I don't know dear, if only they would give us a morsel before we faint away.' Her thin little white-haired lady friend tries to twitter an answer. But the fat one, with her white face and pudgy neck plunged in a short white machine-crocheted acrylic cape, has caught the eye of the waitress. 'Let's see miss, what'll it be. A tea no a rice pudding. Better start off with a little lasagna. Noodle soup, too.'

You start to say something, smiling in a very friendly way. Then hesitate. I have a feeling you want to talk about us. You are improving. I wait. You clear your throat and say:

'The situation of waitresses in Plateau Mont Royal is critical. That's why the comrades were sure that, even if you're resigning from the group as a full member, still, as a feminist and fellow-traveller, you might want to help us in this important revolutionary task. Since you're free this month (I'd taken a month from my translation job to write) the organization has suggested you take a job here at the Grill to start a union organization drive among the staff.' Silence, then: 'I'm sure you'll still have time to write.'

134

At least you have the decency to blush. I feel the black spot rising. For some crazy reason my eye wanders to a pile of your photographs lying on the table. Reminding me if I don't do it, some other admiring woman will. I look closely at the top photo. A pair of legs reflected in a car mirror. Not fat enough for D's. More like the girl with the green eyes. Don't be silly. I've seen legs like that in a million cars parked on a million beaches. Besides, I'm always paranoid in the mornings. If I'm not careful, I'll end up crazy. Like one of those women writing to Juliette in *Le Journal de Montréal*.

> *Chère Juliette. I am 23. He is 26. We're in love, but nearly*
> *every night he stays out late. I wait in my room which is*
> *done in blue silk. He becomes angry if I ask where he's*
> *been. I'm afraid to go out or phone someone because he*
> *might try to call. Sometimes I'm so depressed, the filth piles*
> *up. That really gets him. Signed. Aimée.*

Your hand is drawing a little map on the Labatt's 50 placemat. Little X's marking the Plateau's all-purpose restaurants, those advertising METS CANADIENS, ITALIENS, CHINOIS on their signs. I think of that surrealist game we used to play when me, the Haitian, and this suburban kid in the beret would meet in a café and throw a coin on the map of Montréal. To find out where objective chance would send each of us for an afternoon of automatic writing. You say the obvious: that the restaurant owner mustn't know I'm working for the union. And the union mustn't know I'm in the left, terrified as unions always are that revolutionaries in the ranks will cause their bureaucracy to lose control.

I order another coffee. The door opens and Marcel the delivery boy enters on the run, his pearl purse over his shoulder and carrying a sprung oversized red thumb straight out at the belt. He disappears into the washroom. You say he'll be helpful. A comrade recently saw him in a tulle dress on The Main. And F-group's analysis of the current political conjuncture says a homosexual is objectively in a position of revolt. Marcel sits at the counter and sips another coffee. He always has one ready. 'Get a move on Marcel,' says the Greek owner's wife. She's sitting behind the cash. 'Oui, trésor,' says Marcel, wiggling his ass. And he adds (for she doesn't know French): 'T'as une face comme le cul d'un âne.'

You pause, waiting for an answer. Something tells me I'm going to surprise myself. If I say no, God help me stick to it. I know, I'll make a chart and every day I stick I'll put another check on it.

I smoke slowly, as if I'm thinking. The door opens. In comes Irene, the waitress. She's been out washing the window off. First soap, then cloth, then paper towel. But just as she came in, a big truck went by splashing slush on it and she had to go out and do it again.

Now Irene is waiting on a client. Smiling at him with her madeup tired face and dyed hair. Somewhere finding energy.

'Hallo there longtime no see yessir one Molson coming right up. How's your truck: How you like driving in all this snow? Nice shirt you're wearing. Let me feel. Ohhh. Oh. Mmmm. Lovely material. Me? Okay. A little tired. Don't know what's wrong with me these days. No energy. You don't like my hair you say? Needs something softer? Well, I took this auburn colour because I'm completely grey. You'd never guess, eh? Big storm coming later, I hear? Don't know how you drive on a day like this. Really, what time you finish? You're not going under the Lachine Tunnel, are you? This terrible bus strike and all. Those damn unions. And my kid way over there on the other side of the city. If the storm comes I'm afraid I'll never get home to her. You're really looking good. New haircut, too, eh? Oh I forgot. I'm not supposed to get on the seat like this with clients. Heh heh. Just washing the windows, boss. Forgot to take the fish out of the freezer, too. Don't know what they'll eat without me there. Hold on. Marcel's giving me the eye. Nobody takes better care of their customers than I do. And all this pressure to parlez the ding dong. You don't care, do you? Why should you, you speak both. Main thing is we understand each other. Hey, don't do that, move your hand. The boss. What was I saying? Oh yeah, with the bus strike a ride under the tunnel these cold nights would sure be appreciated.'

Your green spotted eyes are watching me.

I smile wanly, wondering you if get the message.

Somebody puts a quarter in the jukebox. First it lights up, then the snow starts to fall on the scene in the little ball on top. And Hank Williams comes on singing:

Goodbye Joe me gotta go meo myo
Me gotta go pole the pirogue down the bayou ...
Jambalay, and a crawfish pie, an' a filet gumbo.

Free Woman and the Shadow In The Bank

There's a sound like a huge crack (spring breakup on the Castor River back in Lively). The heroine steps through. On the other side the colour's grey, almost silver. Under the cement arch of the Park Avenue underpass the square grey buildings lean against the black clouds. A Chirico city. A final ray of light slanting off the mountainside fills her with a not unpleasant emptiness.

There are various roads. She starts walking. Soon a hard rain is falling. She thinks of the brownish polluted drops as capitalist and patriarchal. She comes to a restaurant on a corner. One of those nearly-empty places with a couple of longish tables, bare white walls, fluorescent lights and plastic hot-dogs for pictures. Anne, a British feminist with long blonde hair, is inside waiting. The heroine shakes out her damp red curls and sits across from her. Her black sneaker boots so wet from walking it will take coffee to stop shivering. Through the window hovers the great stone l'Église St Jean Baptiste in the grey dimness of rue Henri Julien. She puts her thin hand in her pocket and says to her new friend, grinning wryly: 'I've got something to show you.' It's a picture taken of herself sitting in a gazebo like a birdie in a cage. Grey and skinny, with the collarbones sticking out of her white scoopnecked blouse. And a long unevenly hemmed red flowered skirt. She says sarcastically: 'The last stages of love.' Anne looks at the picture through twinkling blue eyes (Welsh on her father's side), exhales some smoke and says in her soft voice: 'Oh we'll have to fatten you up.' Her incredible pink mouth smiles warmly.

A lonely teenager at the next table in tight jeans, brown hair and heavy makeup puts another quarter in the juke box. Edith Piaf comes on singing *Jeeeuh ne regret-te rien*. The teenager gives it a kick because it isn't what she wanted. Anne takes the heroine in her arms and they begin waltzing among the tables. The legs of the heroine lost in the folds of Anne's long Indian skirt. And her head on Anne's well-padded chest. People were still freer then.

But the music stops. The heroine steps out again. A damp March wind is blowing. She likes to feel it on her face. Walking up St Dominique, she tries to absorb the rhythm of the street. Factory smoke. A ragged hustling queen, dressed like a lady pilgrim except for her lipsticked mouth, which is chewing something sweet. Graffiti strewn on walls like music notes. LE MONDE SUCE. O-i-i-i-i. I'M COOKING, COCOTTE. O O O. BE CLEAN SHEEP!

The heroine turns west, making a wide arc towards Park Ave. Above the tacky neons, the clouds are racing black. She strolls by the Greek Workers' Centre where one night recently (they were celebrating something) she went in and danced like crazy. Ate lamb, green beans and drank retsina. Talked with a beautiful dark woman about how the socio-political situation in Greece is changing. All the pleasure quickly dissipating a deep inside feeling that even if she left him, he was the one who had *brutally pushed her away*.

Yes she's pleased at how she's recovered from this broken love affair.

She crosses the street. At the fountain in the park a man in a toque, preaching something incomprehensible, holds out his arms to her. High, high above a drugstore, stands a billboard with a little girl in a yellow raincoat on it. She ignores a quick black flash somewhere in her mind. Yes, she's pleased at how she's learning to write over the top of things. Whatever that means.

She laughs and focuses on walking jauntily. Remembering after awhile how some (French) feminists are saying women, gay AND straight, should live together. The better to create, *dans l'absence du mâle,* a culture where the feminine can be reflected whole. Well, it's true she does enjoy getting up each morning without him there. The ritual of throwing open her windows and breathing deeply. Today the light in the park made the new grassblades limegreen under the trees. The blue sky was hard-edged with white clouds as in a hyperrealistic painting. Sitting on the windowsill, she lit a cigarette. Below a woman in a widebrimmed flower-printed hat, with paper sweet peas also pinned on it, propelled her buxom body past. In life before feminism the heroine would have considered her ridiculous. But now she finds such overstated feminine presence in the midst of concrete and urban racket quite delightful. Maybe it is possible to have a set of female (non-patriarchal) standards to judge the world by. (Although she also loves the many facets of the city.)

She could develop this feminine angle for her novel. Of course the process of setting standards is collective, so she'd have to have a community of women. She might even take up the offer Anne made last week in that Greek restaurant which still has Christmas tinsel hanging in its window. Actually their lunch hadn't been as cozy as she'd hoped. First, it was a grey day. And the waitress, whose black skirt ballooned over her bulging stomach, had such a sad face it spoiled the atmosphere. Then, just as the heroine was hoping to launch into a good, nourishing discussion about the relationship between art and feminist politics. Anne's kind round face creased. And she started talking about some pain of love she'd had. How, walking into a room, she'd found *le genou de Claire* in her lover's bed. The heroine felt unreasonably impatient. Sitting there among the plants, with the smell of retsina and the jukebox playing *Never on Sunday,* she was beginning to think she'd have to remind her friend how melodrama, that ubiquitous form of North American culture, is death for feminists. When Anne, a tough woman thank God, wrapped it up by saying: '... to hell with him.' Taking another bite of souvlaki and swallowing her pain at the same time. 'I'll just devote myself to the Women's Shelter.' She munched thoughtfully. Her blue eyes looked up, a little puffy (she'd probably been hitting the booze lately): 'If you wanted to be around feminists more, you could join us. (Ironically.) Now that you've left the left.'

Leaning out her apartment window in the early morning light, an image of the Shelter floats across the heroine's mind. Breezes ruffling a curtained door. And potted plants. The soft contours and bright colours of the dykes and radical feminists working there. Safe and warm so a woman can really be herself. The image is so accurate, that later, entering the Shelter the first time, she gets a sense of déjà vu.

Anne had said: 'Oh, come on. You'd love the staff. There's H, a surrealist poet. And Céline, whose brother's in jail from 1970. Very exotic.' She had taken another bite of souvlaki and concentrated. Over her head hung a faded Christmas bell. 'I know. We'll get money from the Public Works Program to pay you.'

The heroine throws the match from her cigarette over the sill. It floats past an earlybird happy couple going by. The woman has long hair pinned back on one side, long dress, flat Chinese shoes (québécois hippy style, ca 1972). A little round. He, paler, thinner with a short beard, is nuzzling her neck. Obviously crazy about her. Watching them, the heroine gets this feeling of failure in relationships (only briefly). It also comes to her at parties. When feeling shy, she talks too much. Making too many self-conscious little comments. Leaning on the edge of her desk, her ex once said (his vocables cool and round in the grey air): 'You have relationship problems because your personality's too strong.'

But now all that's over, surely she and he can still be friends. If she doesn't sleep with him he can't hurt her.

She smiles slightly. It's amusing that since she has withdrawn sex, people say he isn't seen with other women either. (Apart from the girl with the green eyes, but she's no problem for she has declared herself a dyke.) When he is, she'll have to be careful not to mind too much. She has written in her diary: *He's just far enough away now that I can let down my defences a tiny bit and sense my real affection for him again. Instead of all that energy-sucking resentment. But I cannot permit myself to get any closer. It's too dangerous.*

Behind her the furniture is piled and the walls are being freshly painted. By herself of course. She's into a total reorganization of her life. Soon there will be plants. She's amazed at how quickly her slim form has filled the space vacated by his clutter, his politics, his coming home late at night. When she finishes painting, she'll go to Chinatown and buy a white teapot with roses on it and matching cups. The better to invite her women friends.

The tourist turns onto St Denis. He's been here before. The sloping sidewalk, the high cobblestone terrace to the right unfold before him like a dream. Yeah, mid-70s sometime. He was walking right here with some other brothers and that crazy québécois with the wild grey beard they met in some bar. His T-shirt was covered with Labatt's 50 caps. Said he was a tourist guide specialising in *du tourisme pour révolutionnaires.* He even had a card. They'd walked over here. Up to the right, the guy had said, pointing to the flats on the cobblestone hill, used to live an early félquiste. But he'd been found murdered in Paris. 'Motive unknown,' said the cops. No one believed it.

Oh, my fingers are getting waterlogged. I should pull the plug, make coffee, and sit at my little table. Except that big black crack in the arborite really bugs me. Reminding me as it does my little novel has certain inconsistencies. Given how the heroine's inner time is fractured between light and dark, so she seems to move in circles. Leaning first one way, then the other: the free woman coming up to the city, then the happy lover slowly slowly disintegrating into melodrama, finally the free woman again. Although Cassandra in Greek mythology also began to think of time as circular while lying down contemplating the stars on Troy's cement ramparts. Watching the movements of the heavens, with illuminating points in the dark waste, she realized things go round appearing to repeat themselves, but not really. She was so absorbed in how this observation helped her intuit future possibilities, that she never died from pain of love. (Which history says, in her case, was considerable.) This was partly due to confidence: she was the King's favorite daughter. Also, being a prophet, her angle was the future.

I like that. Using the future as an angle. It fits in with the idea of feminine standards. Still, to get in the mood, I could use a smoother writing table. There was a nice wood one in the flat on Esplanade. Going by there the other day I realized what a fool I was to let the landlord throw me out. But twas the end of our reconciliation (my love) and I was too exhausted to fight back. I used to love how that tree trunk, against a background of green mountain, climbed skyward outside the middle of my window. When things got bad with us, I dreamed the tree trunk was exploding – but with no visible damage to the house. Anyway, walking along the street there the other day, I missed the place so much. Even the frozen grass under the park's trees smelt fresh compared to elsewhere in the city. And turning on Duluth, I saw the same old slogans still crying from the hospital walls: LA NUIT AUX FEMMES; SOS FLQ. Albeit faded.

The nostalgia made me want a coffee. In La Cabane, the artist with the liver line between his eyes (who's always complaining they refuse him grants) was gazing at a Spanish-looking woman at the next table. She, ignoring him completely, began beating her breasts with her miniscule little fists. While staring at me. 'Look,' she shouts. 'He did this,' hitting herself in a quick staccato rhythm. She means her husband, not the artist. 'On fait l'amour tous les jours mais il m'a menti. Il prend des drogues.' She sticks her tiny fingers up her nostrils in a sniffing motion. C-cocaine. She's from Peru. Got blacklisted for a university sit-in, so came here. Married this guy who said he had a good job. Only later did she learn the truth. Now she can't go back and she can't go forward. On top of it all, she misses her mother. This makes her so furious she beats her chest even harder to show me how he treated her when he came home that morning. I love how her hurt does not prevent her anger. Here is a woman with good orgasms.

Still, the heroine wouldn't let orgasms hold her to a man. Knowing as she does a woman can find other ways to transcend the emptiness. Under an April blue sky, she smiles slightly as she strolls, hands in pockets, small breasts under her Indian shirt, towards the sweet smell of a cookie factory. Next to it stands the Battered Women's Shelter where she's working. The place has a secret address, the better to hide the victims from the husbands. Yet in the end, a lot of the clients return to the bastards. Her expression alters as she remembers how he used to kill her with his vagueness. Making her stoop so low that once she even locked him in, the better to get him to talk. But their conversations were always the same. The air damp with tears and him: mute. She'd make an accusation just to break the silence: 'You're trying to rubber stamp me. To make me say "yes" to your fucked up idea of a relationship.'

Him: The thing I can't stand is

Her: You see my feelings pouring out, just raining, then they come up against this brick

Him: Your questions. Always How come this and How come that

Her: My body's just crying for tenderness

Him: It's none of your business where I am

Her: Yet you say it's beautiful, sexy, fits like a glove

Him: I can feel your resentment pouring out

Her: I'd like to be able to phone you when I'm alone

145

Him: There's always something wrong. These urgent phone calls.

Above her the gargoyles with their round mouths look like they're blowing bubbles in the air. She laughs. At last, she's caught him in his own contradiction. He can't ask her why she's withdrawn from sex because he's always refused to explain anything like that. Of course she's not completely impermeable yet. To prepare for any eventuality, she has even written in her diary: *I feel so good, it scares me. Because I know he'll try to get even by announcing he's found someone more important. I'll just have to be careful not to give in to such psychological abuse.* She walks faster towards the warm coffee in the Shelter office. Sniffing the air. So clear, so damp. In this city spring's as fast as an orgasm. That word again. There is a tightness in the stomach. What's it from? What's it from? She can feel it under her drawstring pants. Feminist style, loose between the legs, so the crotch can breathe.

Maybe the pain is from the exterior. She has this acute awareness of reality that penetrates her. In front of the tenements she's passing (probably built by some Frenchman from Marseilles, for they have large interior Mediterranean courtyards) a group of blackdressed immigrant women are drawn together in a tightknit circle. They're reading a letter. She knows what's in it. A friend of hers has the same landlord: *Dear tenants: Due to the slum conditions these buildings over time have fallen into, we're happy to notify you there will be renovations. You must therefore move by July 1. Tenants failing to comply will have their heat, water and electricity cut off. But we are happy to offer you preferential options if any of you wish to sign for one of our new luxury condominiums. Signed D. Rose. L.L.D. C.A.*

She climbs the Shelter's outside stairs. She opens the door. The walls are peach. Going in here always reminds her of a dream about sex. Don't be silly. It must be the colour. The subject of the staff meeting is: How to keep them (the clients) from returning to their battering men? The door almost hits the cop's

146

wife, who is kneeling in her flowered bathrobe scrubbing the floor. He gave her a slap and threw her from his car onto the dusty road. So her story goes, with emphasis on the dust. Now she's driving the clients crazy, always on hands and knees, scrubbing after them. From the kitchen, a woman in a tight T-shirt (whose husband tried to prostitute her) beckons with hungry eyes.

The heroine just pretends she doesn't see. She knows her attitude needs some work. But occasionally, there's such an emptiness in her she can't handle speaking to a battered woman. They're so depressing. She slams the office door behind her and leans, panting, against the wall.

GREAT. In a shaft of light, Violette's brown head is bent over spread-out cards, telling fortunes. Céline's beautiful ruined face, in profile, watches tensely. Beside them, H, with her wild auburn curls, is pasting a fence of blue eggshells around a poem she's written. The heroine moves closer. Violette spreads her cards deftly in the small space, bounded by typewriter, pot of crocuses, ashtray, coffee cup. Back in St Adolphe they call her *la sorcière*. Because once, while reading her brother's cards, she knew his wife had driven off the road into a deep stream before the cops came with the news. 'I'm next,' says the heroine. In the corner of her eye, W's legs with glistening fair hairs and mauve sneaker boots are disappearing up a ladder on the balcony to fix the roof.

Violette shuffles. The heroine leans forward, nursing a coffee. Vaguely aware she shouldn't do this, now she's a free woman. What? A blue-eyed king and a blue-eyed queen. Violette shakes her head and says: 'It's your ex and some fair-skinned woman. Your own dark-eyed queen of clubs stands painfully at a distance.'

'Hosti de masochiste,' cries H suddenly swirling on her chair. Under her sky blue eyes, her freckles are outrageous. 'You're crazy. When I found my guy with a woman, I just grabbed her by the sweater. And I told her: "Si ça continue, je te tue."' She's laughing her head off, her small waist shaking in its tight band and a hand-made cigarette between her finger tips. Then they notice W standing there, looking furious. She's a dyke, so none of this melancholic heterosexual shit for her.

'Look,' she says, 'we've got work to do.'

'Relaxe un peu,' says H. 'We were waiting for you. If we'd started without you, you wouldn't be happy either.'

W smiles a little. (At the shelter they're proud of how well they deal with any bad vibes between them.) She's just pissed off because there's a new client and no one's looking after her.

The heroine jumps up (the client's hers) and leaves the office. Through a partly opened door she sees a woman sitting on the cheap chenille bedspread folding neat piles of little clothes. Beside her two adorable curly-headed little boys play on the floor. Damn, she's smoking pot. One of those. Well, the heroine won't deal with that tout de suite, shaky as she is from Violette's cards. In a few minutes she'll have her sense of toughness back again. The woman looks up. My God she's beautiful with her brown skin, long brown hair, and solid yet not heavy body. What origin? Irish with a touch of Indian? 'Hello,' says the woman, her voice husky, as if bold yet nervous at the same time. 'The name is Polly. Like a smoke?'

The silver cigarette box proffered is full of fat, beautifully rolled joints.

On St Denis, the tourist stops. There's a blizzard. Snow swirling like ice angels between the steeples. Depositing its lode in long stains on the bar and restaurant windows that line the sloping sidewalk.

Oh God, look at my fingers. They're so waterlogged, I really must get dried and start the novel. The heroine and her friends moving towards the future. Just now that Dr. Schweitzer was on the radio again. Saying Miss Beauchamp's speech turned round and round in clauses dependent on what could have been but wasn't, due to her getting stuck between some inner vision

148

(the desire for a lover's touch and what it represented, which maybe wasn't a lover's touch at all) and the outer world. So that time and space were in a knot. Soon I'll reach my arm out and turn him off. He hates women.

Anyway, in the spring of 79, the heroine and her friends were more like Miss Beauchamp's wild side. I mean when her knot would burst into hallucinations of incredible beauty (Schweitzer had to admit it). And she would start doing anything she pleased, with no regard whatever for social conventions. An outstanding example of this was the girl with the green eyes. She had an air of total self-absorption: getting up each morning, stretching her big toe, then doing exactly what she felt like, without listening to authority of any kind, past or present. Once I met her early on Ste Catherine St., a white knit hat over her short golden curls, her mysterious smile and a way of walking well back (so the pelvis protrudes) on her flat-heeled shoes, indicating certain women never never never will be slaves. Naturally I presumed she was coming from the warm bed of some stunning woman (dark and full-breasted). And I found her so beautiful, so free. That's why (my love) I was so surprised when I saw the two of you from my taxi one year later, walking along Esplanade-on-the-park like birds in paradise.

Shhh, never mind that. I'm using another angle now. Besides, everybody gets what they need. *Although you can't always get what you want.* Those also were my thoughts this afternoon watching Marie through my partly-opened bathroom door in the Waikiki Tourist Rooms. On the sofa her back was slightly turned. I caught a glimpse of how her bra cut the flesh under the back of her white silk dress somewhat below her perfectly straight Clara Bow haircut. Showing that maybe her trick of wearing outer social expectations as a mask, the better to be her own (inner) woman, cost her something. But what I couldn't get over most, lying in my little tub, was how we seem so different. When in the height of the feminist period, on that road to St. Antoine-sur-le-Richelieu for a giant women's party, the harmony was perfect.

149

Twas a beautiful June day and the quality of light was clear. Albeit (my love), walking down the outside stairs through dappled leaves, I felt your shadow standing over us. That was because you'd come to babysit little Marilù who was staying for a week. But for a moment I sensed your nice bulge nestling comfortably in your cut-off shorts. And your shirt open to your waist. The handsomest revolutionary male around. What saved me was knowing that as you watched us leave, you imagined Marie and I had something going on.

Arm 'n arm, Marie and I stepped over the sidewalk, sticky-sweet with a piece of melting gum, and entered her Renault. In the light breeze we drove along, passing the wall mural where the cops are hiding behind bushes waiting to bash some St Jean Baptiste celebrators. The sky was airy blue. We floated through the dusty quarter by Pont Jacques Cartier where that little boy was kidnapped for prostitution. Marie's window was open. Going over the bridge I noticed her silken hair against her cheek. The same colour as my mother's. She tossed it back, laughing perversely.

We're lost the minute we leave the city, miles from the farm where some women are throwing a huge party. She stops the car. I get out and cross a farmer's lawn to ask directions. Due to lack of familiarity with the rural accent, I get it wrong. Already, the afternoon is waning. Back in the car, taking one more false turn, and thinking we're lost for the night, I wonder about the smell of cunt. Behind (my love) your full shadow stands in the summer sun. No, block that out. The car is going over an old road full of curve-roofed houses built in another century. A sign says some Patriotes lived here. Hung in 1837. The fate of marginals. Despite a strange odour and the uncertainty in the air, I'm not worried. No, I'm not afraid, for we take another turn. And the pink mist rising off the river indicates we've found our way at last. We drive through a pair of huge black trees with rather funny leaves. I look again. Although it's summer the trees are bare. The funny leaves are flocks of crows. Reminding me of the black maples under which a skinny little girl is walking back in Lively. In her white dress her body smiles with some thrilling memory. Walking along she tries to put it in a story. But a woman watching from the verandah says: 'Ask the Lord if you're doing the right thing.'

STOP. Where does this guilt come from? I move closer to Marie. Her pink lips are parting in an expectant smile. Instead of two black pillars, Marie sees women dancing laughing telling stories in a circle. Around the huge fire in the field are also little girls. At first I keep an English distance. That's a joke. Yet even from behind I see that everyone is beautiful, albeit dark, blonde, fat, skinny, 15 years or 80. We all grow silent as one rich voice rises above another. Women telling their stories. I move closer.

A lesbian in an embroidered shirt is saying: 'C'est vrai que symboliquement on n'existe pas.' The flames carve out her handsome features. 'La preuve c'est que la fillette de ma chum m'a appelée "Papa" pendant longtemps. On avait beau la corriger. La petite insistait.' (Here some women laugh and some look angry.) She has the sweet smell of women who don't eat meat. Behind our circle is the fertile odour of ripe hay. The rhythm of their voices hypnotizes, almost. All the soft skin and hair around me making me think of Easter as a kid. That's when Georgina's Sunday School girls would climb up the hill with painted eggs and hot chocolate. To watch the sun rise while we meditated on the true nature of Christ's rising. We huddled together, our freezing cotton crotches squatted on the ground. While the sky behind McLaren's barn grew increasingly scarlet. What I loved was how the blush faded into dark blue as the sun rose. And an early bird careened across the sky despite the cold. Then our thoughts turned to the chocolate in the thermos. Of course, we had to wait until Georgina in her pink powder and boned corsets finished praying that our budding youth would hold the promise of the resurrection. Some of us already had our period. I was glad the Easter story was equally for girls.

Marie and I drive back through the gate. A friend of hers is in the back seat. The crows are gone. The tree skeletons have melted into the beautiful night sky. In the distance shines the city. Around us the cement walls of the raised Boulevard Métropolitain. Marie holds my hand between us on the seat. At Boulevard des Sources, the tense voice in the back says: 'You can let me out here.' She'd phoned and phoned her man. Now she ran off along the shoulder, hoping he had finally come home.

The stars shine up above. We drive on. I look at Marie's profile against the background of city lights shining through the rolled-down window. Thankful that we'd found another way to pose the question. We're heading towards Boulevard St Laurent on Le Métropolitain: a crummy shopping centre, gas stations, lower down a ball park and seminary. Something tells me not to, but I ask anyway. 'Vivais-tu le divorce comme une force libératrice?' Suddenly our harmony is shattered with unexpected anguish.

'Liberating,' she shouts. 'Divorce is a simple question of survival. Car il a détruit mon rapport avec mon corps. Nights he snuggled up to me for heat only, never love.' I smiled, feeling superior because sex was something I could ask you for (my love). If we were still together.

'One month after he leaves,' she adds, angrily steering the Renault between two high walls of an underpass, 'he's living with someone else.'

My breath catches: 'Had he uh, been having an affair?'

'That's not the point, bon dieu. The point is, a man can replace one woman with another just like that.' She takes both hands off the wheel and gives them a sliding clap together. 'Dans ce sens ils sont profondément immoraux.'

How silly of me. Of course, she's right. Leaning over, I try to calm her down. Caressing her soft hair. My alabaster cheek against her olive one. At the flat on Esplanade, we kiss goodnight (brushing perhaps too quickly over the mouth). I step out of the car. The beam from Place Ville Marie shines over the park. With her watching my beautiful slim back with the slightly protruding hip I slip through the lattice of leaves and into the dark yard.

Our lips had the taste of wine on them. In the summer of 79.

It's later than I thought. So dark I can't see the clouds bank through my small green window. But I can hear that crazy woman in the next room. Talking all the time while pacing the floor in front of her door. *Body in the river police say the pimp under the cow mural un simple soldat lost Bourassa hot smell by the Cartier bridge....* She told the pharmacist she's afraid of the night. Ever since those junkies came in and stole her things at the Park Avenue rooming house where she used to live. I don't think it's the night she fears, but something else. Like that Guatemalan woman I read about in the paper. She used to worry because her little girl had to inch her way along a kind of strap to get over a deep-gulched mountain torrent on the way to school. Every day the mother thought: 'She'll fall in. I'll never see her again.' Then one day it happens. The kid doesn't return. Turns out she was abducted on the road near the gulch by several men. When her mother heard the news, her reaction was: 'What a fool I was to fear the wrong thing.'

Like me (my love). For all during the reconciliation I thought the competition for your affection was a beautiful swimmer from Vancouver you met somewhere. Then I spy you and the girl with green eyes walking like two love-birds along Esplanade-on-the-park. And seeing the way she's changed, I know suddenly it's her who got the silver plate because she wanted it more than me. This doesn't ease the pain. When I meet Marie and her friends the modernist writers a few minutes later at that gay bar with the little cupid holding grapes in front of a mirror, one of them says (after hugs, kisses and all the little attentions you never get in English):

'You're so white. As if you'd seen a ghost.'

I laugh and say: 'I'm okay. Just looking for another way to pose the question (my lips closing over the long-stemmed glass

153

of Martini Rossi). So I can create a heroine who's not a loser for my novel.'

'And what does that mean, not a loser?' asks Alain. He's a film critic.

'Somebody who's not afraid. Parce qu'elle sait que celle qui perd, gagne,' I answer bravely.

'Not afraid?' asks Alain. 'Isn't that a bit silly, considering the age we live in?'

'I guess I should say someone who can trace where the fear comes from. So it doesn't end up getting sprayed over everything.'

On this subject, the heroine tries to be as lucid as possible in everything she does. Example, walking out of the Shelter office to look after the new client. And half an hour later walking back, forcing herself to sound cool while announcing to the staff:

'Eh, les girls, you aren't going to believe this. But this woman says her old man's mafia. And he might cause us trouble if we keep her.'

Somebody says: 'How titillating, I never thought the Mafia was real.' And they all laugh at the thought of some adventure in this energy-sucking job (a lot of them are artists). Then W says they maybe should, just the same, as a measure of prudence for the sake of the other clients, collectively assess the situation. Therefore, in the yellow kitchen after dinner we gather round the table. Nelly from Nova Scotia contributes a new fact: 'Girls, guess what, I answered the phone about five minutes ago. And the guy says (here she screws up her freckled face to look like a pug-nosed bouncer):

' "Uh, I hear yah got Polly. Me 'n a coupla guys'll be over later to show you broads what's what." '

They all look at Polly. Grinning a little less than they were before. Especially the heroine, who's on night-shift. The corners of Polly's lips turn up sardonically. She says: 'That pet shop he runs is just a front. What do I care who knows? He put us in that trailer out in the country with no money for gas. Just enough food to keep me and the kids going for a week. But sometimes he'd get so carried away with that broad he's got living in our home in Dollard, it's got beautiful light-green wall-to-wall broadloom, he'd forget to come. The kids were starving. That's how come he caught me peddling uppers and downers. The bastard. He'll use it on me if he can. If he doesn't kill me first. I know too much.' Her look around the table implies that now they know too much too. Someone's lip twitches. Polly's brown gaze doesn't miss it. 'You're also scared,' she says, smiling with satisfaction. 'I can see it.'

'Never mind that,' says W quickly. 'What d'ya mean, the pet shop's just a front?'

'Dope,' says Polly. 'They ship it in from Morocco by the ton. Actually I met him on a beach there. Agadir. I don't even know if the oldest is his. I might have been pregnant already.'

Later, the heroine strolls into the living room. Thinking (because joking always helps): This is the city. Eleven PM. Outside, between the crack in the gold brocade curtains somebody donated, rises the full moon. Looking cold despite the weather. The clients are tucked away safe in their beds. The trick is not to panic. The heroine sits on the sofa. Leafing through the dusty feminist pamphlets spilling off the second-hand end tables. The clients hardly ever read them. Except for the cop's wife, none of them cleans up either. They're too depressed. She doesn't blame them. Fear has a way of paralyzing everything. To stay calm, she'll focus on something nice.

Oh, Agadir. (Why not? On that trip to Morocco, my love. Just before we head north to Algiers, we lie in its sun and warmth. Above us they've hardly rebuilt the village after that terrible earthquake. You scarcely see any Moroccans. But down a ways is a colony of American hippies. They leave dirty toilet paper and tampax in the bushes. One morning I find one of them doing a weird ritual on the beach. He has a little penis-shaped black ebony statue. About eight inches. Up close I see it is a woman. 'Black Rosa,' he says, looking up at me. Before caressing her and sticking her in a fucking motion into the sand.)

What's that sound? The heroine's bare feet that were curled

up under her rapidly hit the floor. A click, click. Then ... nothing. She gets a flash of her bloody corpse laid out (before she has published too) on the rug. This is funny. NO, she won't give into fear. Instead of wasting precious time (if something happens, it happens) she opens her black book and jots a note from some reading she's been doing: *They signalled the death of the nature god Pan just as Christianity was about to be victorious.' From Michelet's La Sorcière, comparing that Greek period to the later one when witches were destroyed by the Age of Reason.* All her feminist friends are reading it.

She hesitates and writes again: *He's well in the background now. Just good friends. He's sympathetic when I'm down. Sometimes I wish he didn't need so much from a woman that it takes two to satisfy him. Actually the scarring process is progressing nicely.* There it is, that noise again. It MUST be something in the street. Oh God, something in the street that's walking up the stairs. Her friend Marie's words are ringing in her ears: 'Il faut écrire. Prends pas cette job de militante.' She's so scared, she feels like shitting as the door bursts open and Anne comes in. She says: 'Greater friendship hath no woman than this.' And laughs. Tossing her long blonde hair back over her shoulders the way she does. Taking the heroine in her arms and giving her a hug. Then filling glasses with the brandy she's brought in her bag. Putting some music on. *Oh moon of Alabama. It's time to say goodbye.*

'Oh, not that,' says the heroine, pretending to wince.

Anne (settling on the sofa, a cigarette between her perfect pink lips): 'To change the subject, what do you hear from Jon?'

The heroine (albeit pushing down the memory of Violette's cards): 'D'you know, my not sleeping with him is driving him nuts. And he can't ask why because everyone does what they want. Ha ha I've really got him this time.'

Anne's face clouds briefly, but she only pours another drink, then launches into some fairly humouristic story about her and her lover having a hair-pulling match on Jeanne Mance. While the Hassidic Jews returning home from synagogue in their black silk hats walk gingerly around. Because she'd gone over and found Claire in bed with him again. 'I said if he could do it with her he could bloody well come home and do it with me as well. Finally he did. Left her waiting up there. But nothing happened. He couldn't get it up.'

The heroine's astounded. How could she be so generous with her body when a guy behaves like that? It's true she's the kind who can forget everything and really take off. She even said once that at seventeen, she found out if she turned the cross with the pink ribbon over her bed in Manchester to the wall, she could really come. In fact she couldn't stop.

'Anyway,' cracks the heroine out loud. 'Why are two feminists crying over spilt milk?'

They must have been getting drunk. Because they start laughing at that wonderful dirty joke. And it's not until the chilly red dawn that the heroine opens her eye on the sky blushing between the crack in the curtains. And thinks (for some crazy reason): EASTER.

They step into the street with the energy that follows une nuit blanche. Past the cookie factory the air smells sweet. Up a path covered with old leaves to the mountaintop with its cross. Arm'n arm. Through a dale where the new buds trim the boughs with pale green lace. Emerging at a chalet. Birds are singing with the tenderness of spring. From a bench on the chalet's verandah they let their ruined faces warm like stones in the sun. Behind them some wooden squirrels sit silent in the chalet's rafters. An old man with a magnificent cane goes by singing the praises of Israel. Watched, with cat's eyes, by a young guy in high boots and long coat (like a German officer, ca 1930). The heroine's head seeks out her friend's chest, so wide and solid. But Anne's saying: 'We better get a move on.' She means, to catch the bus for the abortion march on the Québec National Assembly. They're announcing thousands of women. Perhaps the biggest one in history. Climbing down the mountain towards the city, Anne says thoughtfully: 'Problem is, we're stuck with new men. The rare ones who make love right and help around the house, so every woman wants them.'

'Not lesbians,' answers the heroine. But the black spot rises.

157

She pushes it down, the better to hide the king and blue-eyed queen. 'Shhh,' she adds as they arrive at Parc Jeanne-Mance where women are running to catch the bus, 'we have to enjoy every minute.' They survey the scene. Bright sweaters. Bottoms of all shapes. Multi-coloured sneaker boots. Hair of every colour fresh and shiny in the April air. The heroine admires the down over a rosy lip. And other sensuous mouths under flying banners that read: NOUS AURONS LES ENFANTS QUE NOUS VOULONS.

Yes, sisterhood is paradise. She snuggles under her coat, taking in the ripe-sweet smell of women on a bus. By the side of the road grass speeds past. And flowers pushing through the gravel with the energy of early summer. Behind them a friend of W's, all tensed up about something, swallows valium. An Italian woman balances on the arm of her chair, telling about a women's occupation of a Roman castle. They set up a whole community in it. Abortions on one floor, battered women on another. And on the top floor a newspaper called *Quotidiano Donna*. When the fascists attacked, they just unleashed their Doberman pinschers on them. (One dog for each of the 13 doors that surround the courtyard.) 'Après ça,' says the woman, pushing back a long tress of silkbrown hair, 'tout était tranquil.' Everybody laughs. The bus bumbles on past St Hyacinthe (known for its apples), past Drummondville (for its pianos), towards old Québec. The heroine stretches out, feeling good as always when surrounded by the energy of women. Yes, sisterhood is … excellent.

Oh, Sepia. What destructive devil suddenly made me swing round and ask W's friend where the girl with the green eyes was?

'Didn't you know?' After all those pills W's friend's eyes are finally nonchalant behind her glasses. 'She's gone to the country with Jon and Marilù.'

I'm ashamed to say I snapped back: 'Well where's her sense of feminist duty? This is supposed to be our most important demo.'

W's friend shrugs. 'Maybe she felt like it. I know it doesn't seem right. But at this point she's trying to control her life.'

I sit back, overwhelmed with such betrayal. How could she abandon her sisters to spend a day with you, my ex? Beside me I see Anne's face is white with sadness. For me, for all of us. To cheer her up, I crack out of the corner of my mouth:

'Brecht never said what Mother Courage did for sex.'

The tourist continues down St Denis. He steps into a large café built around a courtyard. By the fire, a frozen smile. A finger unwinds and points at his cigarette package. He offers one to the young woman, whose lips are purple. An old bag in a filthy suede skirt is half sitting on the woodpile. He has a flash, as if he's seen her somewhere before. Anyway, the smell is unforgettable. She's mumbling to herself in English against the cacaphony of French. Her words sound like a bad cartoon (looney tune, he thinks) about the north: *when she fell through the river ice, they were not at all content I pulled her back again they would have preferred that she never went through it's true that after she was never the same she saw everything backwards*

She stops.

The tourist, *faute de quoi faire*, prods her a little: 'Then what?'

She looks through him and says: *her mother, the music teacher, poured tea on the frozen spot.*

I've got to get out of the tub right this minute. Because listen, there's someone at the door. The welfare woman. No, it's too late. Dope-crazed junkies. Shhh, don't be silly. My heart's beating so loud I can't hear anything. Try and listen...

Nothing. I'll have to watch the paranoia. The heroine of the novel has the same problem. She just can't seem to march on the bright hard edge of future very long without the dark side creeping up on her. Sepia, what if for some women utopia isn't natural? Cassandra saw the dark side, too, blaming it partly on the march of history. She didn't mince her words about it either, which is why she wasn't popular. Summer nights, pour combattre ce vide, the heroine and her friend Anne drink in various cafés. In one of them (August, 79) a black clown appears. His act consists of trying and trying to get his limp little white rope to stand up. It keeps falling down. The two women roll their eyes and move to the terrasse outside.

It's so hot, they're drinking diabolo menthe. Over their heads a jet suddenly appears, uncharacteristically low in the black night sky. 'Skylab,' chime several clients in unison. They're wearing loose shirts and light trousers instead of jeans, in the spirit of the coming decade. One of them explains that on the news at 6 PM they announced a falling Russian satellite will touch the earth tonight somewhere in Canada. 'Chicken littles, we are,' says Anne. 'The sky is falling in and we don't know where.' The heroine says thoughtfully: 'I can see how we women might one day create something entirely new. I mean it's true there's something in women that spontaneously refuses militarily-oriented space races and torn holes in the ozone layer. No doubt our desire to nurture children. Problem is, individually, how do we definitively keep reality from penetrating and fanning the despair in us?'

Anne says quietly: 'I guess we just keep trying. Collectively. We have to maintain a protective circle.' Then she says to the waiter: 'Non, pas un diabolo menthe; UNE CRÈME DE MENTHE. Sur glâce. Make it a double, please.'

Oh, I wish I'd asked Marie that question about melancholy versus progress in a modern heroine. I mean could the heroine, in the whole picture, lean even more to darkness than to light? Becoming a tragic figure? We could have had one of those interesting conversations like we used to have Sunday afternoons in that St Denis St. café. With coffee bubbling, music playing, and in our favourite, a fire burning reassuringly in a corner fireplace.

Yes, I should have got out of the tub and sat on the sofa beside her. We could have even ordered in some dinner. Poulet bar-b-que, pizza, submarine sandwiches, mets chinois, spaghetti, or lasagne. I suppose none of that would please her. Anyway, she changed the subject just as I was about to ask. I even turned off the water the better to hear. For a minute the room was deadly quiet. A drip fell softly. The green light put her at a distance. Then she said: 'For no one else would I do this. My film is in its final editing. Do you know what that represents? But people say you're in a bad way. Dis-moi que tu commences à être un petit peu moins déprimée.'

I lifted my leg out of the tub and examined it thoughtfully. Wanting to point out she had a role in this. That when my image of cool, exotic anglaise (i.e. fair curls, a cute accent, and genes imprinted with the formula of success) began to tarnish, she lost interest. When I got pneumonia she didn't mother me. When I was headed towards the disastrous reconciliation, she didn't try to stop me. No, she may have inadvertently encouraged it. For she came into the flat on Esplanade just after we (my love) got together again for the last time. And seeing me lying there, waiting for you to come, in my white sweater and long red skirt on the cushions on the rug, she said: 'So you've done it. Well, if you have to you have to. Vis-le au fond. And above all, don't forget to write it.' She didn't need to tell me that. I had just started a new section in the black book called: UNDER THE LINE OF PAIN. In which I'd written: *Hélas, we're back together again. A little tipsy one night and ... now we're 'together' but with 'no commitments.' Your terms completely. I guess my problem is, physiquement t'es le genre qui me plaît.*

Never mind, this is the 80s. Some even call it post-feminist. Outside white snow glows like Roxy paint under the black night. Oh. The ripples jerking up the stomach. Don't stop. Get it while you can. Damn. Just a tickle. After I always feel like crying. Then some starving Africans walk across the television screen. Reminding me that in larger contexts, North America is like a soap opera for the white and educated. The heroine, to balance her particular brand of pain, must constantly strive to find other forms in life and art to express the diffuse and varied tones of poetry in her. That's why, when she can't sleep (although it's less often now, for Polly has relieved tension at the Shelter by fleeing to Vancouver), she takes long walks to study the graffiti and other night images. ONLY THOSE LEFT STANDING WILL HAVE TO FALL. ABOLISH MONEY, FREE THE COMPUTOR, FEMMES VIOLENTES. Or the guy leaping out of the flower market toward her, before suddenly veering off into the dark. Against a background of the rhythmic screech of cars with their glaring lights. And hundreds of black tires piled up against a garage wall.

One November morning she opens her eyes and thinks (without knowing why): this is a turning point. She writes in the black book: *Seems to me this should be a nice date. I do believe at last a metamorphosis is taking place. Found a rhythm for my short story about the kid and her shoplifting mother. That of a car idling unevenly – because they're on the run. Hurrah. And what if, in a story, the words had equal value for their sound and even colour as for their 'meaning'?* While waiting for her expresso coffee pot to bubble up, she thinks of an old Indian her grandfather knew. He'd watch her boyfriends walk by his shack (near the railway tracks at the edge of Lively). With one glance he'd read their faces. As if lips and eyes and nose were another kind of language. And tell Grandpa everything about them, past and future. She smiles as she sips her coffee. Feeling good.

The only disappointing note is her slightly scratchy throat. Also that errand she has to run before she starts her morning's writing. Walking to the bank she notices the sky has a flat and shiny quality, like a knife. Opening the bank door, she senses the air inside is thin as cellophane. The woman next in line, with hooked nose, curly hair, and coat open over enormous breasts, immediately starts talking. Complaining about how the bank is exploiting ordinary people with its long lines. Eventually she discloses her father was a socialist journalist in Vienna.

The heroine nods sympathetically. Wondering if she should share that private fantasy where she walks into the manager's office. And butts her cigarette in his hand when he sticks it out to shake.

Except the woman's getting nosy. 'What do you do?' The heroine replies briefly to show her disapproval. 'So you're a writer are you? I write at night and on holiday in Morocco.'

'Yeah,' says the heroine, out of the side of her mouth: 'Well you'll have to watch out for those Arab guys.' The woman says she'll watch out alright. She loves them. They're so beautiful, so willing. Especially the young ones. 'I mean really young. The way they nibble at your ear.'

The heroine can't help smiling again. In fact a vision of sex on the beach at Agadir rises out of the thin air of the bank. Or is it some other association? Oh God, oh no, it's Polly shuffling by. How come she's here and not out in Vancouver?

'What happens next?' W asked later, sitting at the table in the bleak albeit yellow Shelter kitchen. The heroine coughed and answered:

'Polly looks at me with her dead expression. Her body's leaning forward, swaying slightly. As if so empty, gravity can't hold it. Then she says: "He got the boys. And now they won't even cash a goddamned welfare cheque for $160." I couldn't believe it. I mean we thought she'd be safe in Vancouver. And it was such a relief when she and the kids got on that bus. We weren't wrong to let her go, were we? How else could she have escaped from Salvatore's thugs?'

W: 'It was her decision. I think we just feel guilty because we were glad to get rid of her. I mean the constant threats from those thugs made it unbearable. I have my ideas, too, about how they got the number.'

The heroine (coughing harder): 'Yeah, none of us could sleep. Anyway, in the bank, I think she saw the disappointment in my eyes. Because she turned around and started shuffling out. You should have seen her. She was wearing a greasy suede jacket and was as slumped over as an old woman. Naturally I followed. We went into that Greek restaurant near the laundromat run by the born-agains. I ordered baklava and coffee for her. She only smoked. A woman who has lost her children only smokes.'

The heroine stops and coughs until she can hardly get her breath.

W: 'Calm down, are you sick?'

The heroine: 'So I ask: "What happened, Polly?" She answers: "What difference does it make?" In such a faint voice, I could tell it hurt to talk. Her face was so white and expressionless. And it took her a long time to get to the part that hurt. She said the kids weren't too bad on the bus, considering the trip took four days. Which was a good thing because she couldn't have managed. Not bad but not good either, the way they've been uprooted lately. After a few days in Vancouver she was sure she'd done it. No sign of Salvatore. She couldn't believe her luck. The place was like paradise with flowers blooming and birds singing. She got a little attic flat (under a false name) with a nice garden. Then one evening the doorbell rings. And he walks in out of nowhere. Without even waiting for her to answer. With him is the driver of a taxi parked below. She fights and screams but nobody comes. It's all over in two minutes. One of the kids is clinging to her, but they just grab him and run. Two minutes and her boys are gone. She finds out later he flew there and back in the same day. She got right on the bus for the long return trip. But she knows she'll never be able to kiss them again.

'I said to her: "Oh Polly, you're just distraught. We'll go to court and get them back." And she said, sarcastically: "Sure, you'll be able to help me now just like you did before." That really got me.'

W: 'Nonsense, we've got that good feminist lawyer.'

The heroine (leaning forward on the table, looking a little weak): 'Polly says no lawyer's any good against the expensive show Salvatore can put on. His boss even has a certain judge completely in his pocket. He'll show up in court in beautiful clothes with his welldressed girlfriend. And tell the judge he's going to marry her to give the boys a family. He'll say Polly left home with the kids to live in that crummy trailer and peddle uppers and downers. He'll even have proof. If she tells the court the pet shop's a front, she's as good as dead. She'll lose custody. And who's going to make him grant her visiting rights even if they're awarded?'

W's almost shaking she's so furious. Her fists are clenched on the table. 'That Polly,' she says, 'defeats herself in advance by her fear of him. How did he find out where she was? Eh? I bet she told that friend who drove her here to the Shelter that first day. Yeah, she probably set herself up by telling someone he could threaten until the beans were spilled. She has to fight to win this time.'

Polly did fight. At least she went through the motions. Watching her stand there in court in her sober skirt (for the image) and neatly combed hair, I couldn't get over how much she seemed like any of us. But Sepia, it all turned out exactly as she predicted.

The tourist walks faster. The snow has nearly stopped. Maybe he'll go to that bagel place after all, it reminds him of New York. He's back on The Main. Through a lighted window he sees a parrot. Behind it on a pale blue bedspread a woman puts a cat between her breasts.

He enters the restaurant called Bagels'. The waitresses have trendy haircuts, black ties and black pants. The radio is playing jazz. On the next stool a young man with a shaved head is colouring a purple-and-white striped placemat black. He uses a felt pen, scribbling furiously. Stopping to stretch his cramped fingers, he says (unsolicited) to the tourist: 'Had the highest IQ in high school. It was after the bad acid trip I decided to become an artist instead of a doctor.' Then bends his head back, colouring darker and darker, harder and harder, more and more obsessively. 'Have to get done with this by 5 AM. That's when Mr. Klein lets me in his pharmacy to scrub his floor. At that hour there are lots of gulls in the park. They're beautiful. Very beautiful.'

Outside, a shadow passes birdlike by the window. The grey woman stops in front of the store next door. Shivering a little. She moves closer to read the sign. STRAWBERRIES FROM SPAIN. Her shoulders shake and shake from coughing.

They say illness in the lungs means sadness. Pneumonia, TB, the cancer from cigarettes people smoke to fill the emptiness. Maybe the pneumonia I got last winter was the cause of the final humiliation. Of course, a real heroine would never get dragged down like that. For, lying in her cold (then hot) bed in her little flat on Esplanade, she'd force herself to think positively: 'I'm doing great, if I could just get rid of this damn cold.' Tis November, 1979. Due to her long illness, the kitchen cupboards are getting bare. On the window pane the frost resembles a row of priests holding candles. She watches them grow as the fever rises. Then it plunges so fast she has to take hot baths to warm up. Then cold packs to cool her down. On the radio they're saying a nuclear power station near the border is heating up dangerously. If it ever blew, there could be fallout over Montréal. Or over Drummondville, depending on the weather. Weak as she is she calls Marie and asks: 'Uh have you heard the news?'

'Comment veux-tu que j'écoute les nouvelles?' replies her friend. 'Je suis tellement prise avec mon film.'

Heroine: 'Would you like to come over?' (When Marie says 'yes' she's going to ask for groceries.)

Marie: 'J'aimerais bien. Mais tu sais bien que je n'ai pas le temps. Besides, I can't afford to catch that cold you have. I can hear you breathing over the phone. Shouldn't you see a doctor?'

The heroine hangs up. She would be angry if she had the energy. But Marie angry back could be really scary. The woman has a temper. Still, someone should point out to her that in the inevitable contradiction between sisterhood and the self-focused, egotistical requirements of art, she has chosen the latter. And under the circumstances it isn't fair. True, Anne (who's not an artist) hasn't come either. But that's different because she's in Manchester visiting her family. Lying back on the pillows, the heroine notes how in November the windows darken so terrifyingly early. But she won't let it get to her. On the radio, the authorities are claiming there isn't much radiation danger in the area. Then the environmentalists come on and say they're lying. At night, she dreams of her former lover's nice back. His nice back. It's okay to have dreams like that. Statistics show even strong women have them, when there's sadness from breaking up. Oh, the back's so straight, so cuddly under his blue T-shirt. He also has a wonderful bedside manner (when he really loves someone). Bringing steaming cups of perfect coffee on his blue and white tray. A single maple leaf falls down outside. The heroine's walking outside Polly's trailer in a field of snowmen. On the ground are sparrows pierced with bows and arrows. In the background Mick Jagger is singing: *Angie, Angie, you know I love you / but*

Waking up, the gesture of calling him is barely conscious. He comes almost immediately with a comrade who's a doctor. He's also bearing a fish tank to keep her company. When her pneumonia is better, (he warns) she'll just have to pay for the expensive little motor that keeps the air going through the water. So the fish can breathe. And, she mustn't imagine his coming like this means anything. They're only friends. Falling asleep, the caption of the fever dream is A COLD FISH (as she writes later in the black book): *Something's gnawing at me (impatience? desperation?). I fall asleep and it turns into a fucking fish story. I dream you and Venus, that swimmer from Vancouver they say you've been seeing recently, are standing together in a fish tank. Upright on your fins. All shiny. All silver. It makes me so angry I try to drown you. Then I remember you both like having your head held under water. BECAUSE YOU'RE FISH.*

Shhh, if the heroine keeps up like this she'll be sorry. I'll work better out of the tub. I'll have more distance. Especially if I leave this place and go to one of those all night cafés. What can I wear now that winter's here? The olive-green jumpsuit is kind of thin. Over it I could put the old fur coat that used to belong to Her.

Still, I don't know if a real heroine would do what she feels like doing next. Probably because her resistance is very low. They say pneumonia is often followed by depression, making a person needy for affection. Anyway, she hits an unexpected down, just as she's on the mend, due to a surprise visit from an F-group comrade she used to know. The woman comrade is lying on the floor, smoking a joint and admiring her own short fat foot waving in the air, when she suddenly pronounces a fatal sentence. 'I hear things between Jon and that swimmer from Vancouver are very serious.'

Even in her weakened state, the heroine keeps her cool. Although she knows, with her habit of delayed reactions, her defences might crumble any minute. 'Uh, what's she like?'

'Beautiful. I saw a picture of her. She looks like that statue of Venus rising from the waves.' The heroine says nothing. Just smokes a cigarette (against the doctor's orders), thoughtfully. When Comrade C leaves, she whispers to herself:

'The trick is not to panic. For I don't want him. But it wasn't nice of him not to tell me.

'I need some additional information.'

Due to an early winter thaw, late December, 1979 has that cold damp air hardly breathable. The heroine is waiting in the shadow of a house, her feet in the slush. At last the door of the red brick flat opens (French style, directly on the sidewalk) and he comes out. Followed by the girl with the green eyes. The heroine holds her breath, slipping farther back. Watching as her ex and his platonic friend, the girl with the green eyes, looking less like a woman than like a perfect, rich, latino boy in her short curls and hand-woven poncho, retreat in the night.

But there in the shadow something awful suddenly occurs to her. There's safety in numbers. So if the girl with the green eyes is a dyke, and D (as the grapevine reports) has truly receded from his life, that in fact only leaves Venus. Not that it matters given she, the heroine, and Jon are through. She just has to prepare herself for all the gossipy eventualities. So her face won't slip if somebody comes along and says: 'Oh, have you heard, he is moving to Vancouver, the better to be with her?'

From the corner of the house the heroine watches them move along in the fading light, and disappear around the corner of l'Église St Jean Baptiste (where they still give out *petits pains* to the poor June 24, as in the expression: *né pour un petit pain*). Crossing the street, she thanks God she's working under cover of dusk. The key she has from before turns quickly in the lock. Her feet patter up the dark stairway. She KNOWS there'll be loveletters from the Pacific. Even though he's told her it's a LITTLE relationship. She opens another door. It smells of gas and there's a dirty blue rug on the floor. On the bed, the beautiful scrunched-up colours of an African blanket. (He never buys anything tacky North-American unless he has to.) Antique pine book cases and a blue and white slot machine from the early 50s. Sure enough, in the open bottom drawer of an oak filing cabinet, a letter sticks out. Victoriously, she grabs it. Reading once rapidly for the juicy parts; again carefully, for the nuances.

Dear Jon: I'm so glad we saw each other again. And realized how serious things have grown between us. When you whispered 'I love you' on the phone the other day, it sent shivers all over me. You have the most beautiful body I've ever seen in a man. As I'm athletic, too, we go well together. And politically, I can learn so much. I love your group's let-them-eat-cake theory regarding the effect of organized sports on the ordinary spectator in capitalist society. I don't know what to do. I've never met someone who interests me like you. I keep having these erotic dreams which get interrupted by the alarm for swim practice. Please come soon. We'll go to the mountains or we'll go to the sea... He calls this a 'little relationship'? The woman has nerve, not afraid to show how much she cares. No wonder she's winning (at least that's how the heroine would feel if she and Jon were still together). A man always has to be reassured, no matter how confident he appears.

The heroine puts the letter back in the drawer, trying to remember how it was folded before. Tossed in there as if he'd shown the girl with the green eyes his little trophy. She bets he did. Her body is full of something sugary-vinegary. Glowing with satisfaction because her intuition was right. Yet feeling evil for what she's done. Hurrying down the street, she is dying to tell Anne. She enters the restaurant on the corner with the plastic hot-dog pictures where, earlier, the two of them had danced. Now the jukebox is playing Willie Nelson in québécois. Very sentimental. Anne listens. Then says in her wonderful soft voice: 'I'm afraid reading his letters is only hurting you.'

NO. I can't let her disintegrate like this. Racing towards the final humiliation (the reconciliation) as if she can't resist the blackness in her. It would be better if that dark smudge of desperate need for love after the pneumonia hid something more essential. More socially progressive. Yes, that's it. A sensitive, progressive woman naturally absorbs the pain from the air and from the streets, until it meets up with that sad (unidentified) gap in her own self. The way that children do when those they love are hurt. This even happened once with little Marilù. We were in a Spanish restaurant. And over my café-au-lait I was telling some friend how you (my love) were killing me with your affair. My stomach hurt so much I couldn't swallow. Little Marilù started eating bread. Slice by slice in greater and greater panic. Until she'd eaten nearly the whole loaf. As if trying to absorb a maximum of my pain into her little body.

Anyway, the heroine has decided nothing drastic yet. She'll wait until the pneumonia, that malady of sadness, has run its course. Before plotting a possible return to him. The scene could be his little flat. It's full of comrades. Luckily, she's had a few glasses of cognac. Also her hair looks great: shorter than usual and behind her ears to show the beautiful square lines

of her face. Over her tight jeans, an old tweed suit jacket of her
dead mother's found in a trunk. Tis January, 1980 and she's
knocking on his door. She can tell from the smile on his face he
knows why she's there.

They climb the dark stairs into his kitchen. The comrades
(ex-comrades for her) are drinking from his mother's gift of
Schnapps. She sits on his knee doing imitations of politicians.
Everybody's laughing. They love self-directed females who
aren't afraid. Then, one by one (out of discretion) they get up
and leave. Shielded by the huge plants he put in his kitchen to
hide the view of falling sheds, they start to make love. With her
head against his chest, she smells the faint odour of sweat. Skin
like a girl's except no tits. Exactly what she likes in a man. Her
veins run sugary-vinegary with pain and sweetness. His penis
rises white in the night. She strokes his neck with the hand of a
professional. The better to keep a distance. He's whispering he
loves her, but he just wants to make it clear this time his life
doesn't start and end with her. Never mind that. A woman only
satisfies her needs by standing outside them. She knows how
not to panic if her partner refuses (sometimes) to fill the emptiness in her. When he sees how cool she is he won't fear her.
She will even keep the jealousy (like what she feels looking over
his shoulder at a photo of the girl with the green eyes on the
table) to her diary. As if, in order to survive the 80s, she had to
lie, too. After they have sex (his penis is huge) she goes home,
opens her black book, draws a thick black line in it and gives it
the title UNDER THE LINE OF PAIN. *We are together again.*
My fragility I guess after my sickness. And the knowledge he
was with somebody else drove me to his door. Well received.
Although I can tell he's not totally convinced. I can't stand it,
but I'm pretending to.

No, that isn't right either. Now I'm out. I'll just wrap myself up
in the blanket and sit at that arborite table until dawn comes. A
real heroine wouldn't cover her feelings the better to please a
man. It would only drive her crazy. Unless she's obsessed with

living dangerously. The better to find, in the dark gap behind the hurting masks, the real voice of story in her.

Yes. At first (after the reconciliation) Marie liked the way my lips were swollen with sexual satisfaction. But then she said: 'Tu me fais peur.' (Because every time she came to visit, I was lying on the rug in the dark red skirt, a white sweater, waiting for you my love.) She said: 'Tu vas craquer si tu ne défais pas le noeud. S'il te plaît, FORCE yourself to write it. By your own words you may start to live.' And her heartshaped mouth parted in a slight smile.

Sepia, she's so beautiful when she talks of writing, you can almost feel the edge of freedom. As in a Cocteau film, ca 1940. A woman in a black skirt, black gloves, nipped in waist is walking out a door towards a black and white café. Orpheus waits. From that moment, you know anything can happen.

Jealousy, A Fish Story

This is the line of pain. Like in Doris Lessing's (black) notebook, I think. In my palm I imagine I see happiness, yet I fear what I must pay for this reconciliation.

Jan. ? 1980: Outside, it's cold and white, but dates seem immaterial. I feel so weird, I take sleeping pills, I drink, I want to run away. Like brides feel, I've heard. Their white silhouettes isolated against the dark background of wedding pictures.

The other night it grew mild, and I went out. Crying as I walked. Somehow ending up in St Henri. In a Chinese restaurant I ordered fried rice. Then noticed everybody staring. At first I thought they thought I was a hooker. I said I wanted pills and a woman showed me the doctor's office around the corner. His receptionist said: 'Hello, I'm Jane, the doctor's wife' (staking out her territory). After which the doctor (young and blond and from South Africa) told me I'm having a serious depression. Those computer cards he filled out scare me. I wonder if they give them to the mounties? Outside the doctor's house was a funny little square. With a shiny skating rink over which were strung crazy masks and little lanterns. I don't know what for. The houses around it had turrets, gargoyles, balconies,

173

curved and brightly painted stair railings. As if the architect, ca 1910, was doing acid. Standing there I really felt like part of it.

Later, at home, when you came through the door, I smiled sweetly. Watching myself wanting you so much. As if we were in the theatre.

Outside, still white and cold. Woke up this morning thinking I have to focus on myself (as the shrink at McGill told me). To keep my little ego from folding up like a small triangle in the pit of my stomach whenever we're together. The shrink said a lot of people actually love in triangles, despite the misery it gives them. Because they had to share their mothers with someone, so it's familiar. I said nonsense, the only thing She loved more than me was God. The shrink smiled her personality-girl smile and waited. Sitting back in her comfortable yellow-painted wicker chair from New England.

I am beginning to understand the powers of darkness. After what happened when I heard through the grapevine Venus was on her way here from Vancouver. In fact she was on the plane that very minute. I ran home and dug out of the cupboard a picture of her you'd accidentally left behind. Then, Sepia, just as the plane was about to land, I-I-I burned it. Smiling to myself as the flames engulfed the picture of her sweater, her curls, her horsey chin. Hoping the plane would –. Never mind. This I can't tell to anyone, even Anne. Although I did mention I was interested in witchcraft and she said: 'Me, too. Except I'd be afraid it worked.' I wanted to protest that using blackness in this negative way is the ultimate guile of the powerless. But in a sense she's right. For nobody can exist entirely in darkness any more than entirely in the light.

In that picture you took of me the weekend Venus was coming (it turned out to be a false rumour) I look 40. Wrinkles radiat-

174

*ing up from my dry lips. Dark circles under my crazy unhappy
eyes. Hair wild. Sitting there in a ski sweater, of all things.*

*Feb. 12, so nearly Valentine's Day. After a huge snowstorm
that's quickly melting, you came and sat on my rug. And we
listened to a Kathryn Moses record you'd bought. The lyrics
went something like:* I want to see you smile / even when we're
happy I see your face / and know you're thinking what will go
wrong next. *Her high notes flying madly off the edge reminding me a woman has to be courageous. So I said: 'the pain is
like a grain of dust in an oyster. The layers of pearl are starting
to grow over it into something beautiful.'*

*You said that was very poetic. But you still felt I was pres-
suring you not to be spontaneous.*

I said, uh, what do you mean?

*You said: 'For example what if I said yes, I love somebody
else (too)? You'd go crazy.'*

Oh God what does that mean?

*March 8: Today I woke up feeling furious with your sick atti-
tude regarding relationships. And decided to go for brunch with
an anglophone student I'd met at some demonstration. Flirting
a little to make the situation between you and me more sym-
metrical. The guy is doing a doctorate in a branch of semiotics.
So, we're sitting in a Spanish restaurant on Park Ave. talking
about how the French modernist scene is different than the
English, etc. Smoking cigarettes and drinking Sangria. When
suddenly I can't remember how to get to the end of a sentence.
Each time I start, it's as if the memory of the past (the noun,
the sentence's beginning) wipes out the present (verb). So I can
no longer move forward in the words. This is so scary I run out
of there around the corner to the shrink at McGill. She says
(sitting in her wicker chair): Gail, the problem is you've lost
your boundaries ... Caught as you are between wanting to be
your own self* AND *the object of his affection.*

175

I say that's obvious. But how to define those boundaries yet have love too? She wouldn't or couldn't answer, which really made me laugh.

March 15: Sometimes I think we're going to make it. A few days ago things seemed almost normal, my love, between you and I again. We sat on the edge of your bed talking about a trip you were going to take to Chicago. You said, you would like to take me with you, but.... Then looking at me, you started laughing. I said: Why? You said a streak of very black anger had just passed through my eyes. Making me very beautiful. Naturally a woman has mixed feelings about compliments like that. We took a cab to the Iroquois Hotel to hear Big Mama Thornton sing the blues. Songs like Big Red Rooster.

Back home we made love wonderfully well. You said you hadn't had such a good time since, since – you refused to finish your sentence.

April 4: A bizarre thing happened this morning. I dreamed that the fish couple was dying in the tank. When I woke up the Papa Moon you gave me was really dead.

April 9: Early in the morning. An April rain falling. Sometimes I wish we could go back to when you used to pour out all that tenderness on me. Oh God, I want to wipe out our growth. In the fish dream last night, you were standing on your fins. On second look they were shiny silver boots. I moved even closer and saw the boots were made from silver paper. The caption was FEET OF CLAY. *That was a funny thing to say about a man like you.*

April 13: Grey day as in the film Clockwork Orange. *All that violence, the boys in white beating up everyone. Then outside the cinema, green and orange cars parked. Hate is orange. I realized that very clearly when we had dinner after the movie with two friends of ours who also know Venus. In fact, it was while she was a guest in their house that you fell madly in love with her. So naturally I wanted to be on my best foot. To prove you and I are a better couple (or loving friends, or whatever your new definition of us is) than you and her. At the table I was nervous and euphoric. Trying to keep the conversation going, I got on the subject of how I thought women from your country were too silent despite their sexual freedom. Qu'elles n'avaient pas la parole. And you got mad and said to lay off your family like that. And I said I wasn't really referring to your family, but talking in general. And you went off to the other room to sulk before they even served dessert. I felt so furious at your refusal to validate our couple even a little, every sentence I thought up was like a black drill moving round and round deeper and deeper into the ground.*

April 23: At 2 AM I was in a bar with Anne and some of her coked-out friends. One of them said to me: Be thankful this ain't the suburb of Dollard. Enjoy the agony. And gave me a sniff of what he had to offer. Everything turned blue. Then the colour sepia.

I leaned back on Anne, wearing the dark green wool dress with gold studs across the chest that once belonged to Her. Feeling numb, but relatively alright. Because suddenly I could see how survival for a woman is a little like the negative of a photo. She just has to pick the place in it where night (her deepest self) and day (reality) are combined in the right synthesis of light and dark for her. Even if it's not quite (I started laughing) socially acceptable.

I was laughing. Anne's beautiful lips brushed my ear: I'm relieved, she said, to have you back. Those incredible lips whispered closer: You just went through that silly reconciliation because you're guilty about who you really are. I laughed harder, thinking of Georges Sand. Who once described the space she'd picked by saying (without a modicum of shame): I'm so difficult; that's why I've been through so many men.

Play It Again, S

Dawn. It's snowing out. The street is so quiet, I feel like I've stepped through a glass. Now I can keep the whole picture in my head walking to Bagels' for breakfast. Eggs over lightly. Paprika potatoes. Coffee. Extra bagel to keep me going. So where was I in the story?

Oh, yes.

This is the city. November 1, 1980. Five AM. Suddenly the little girl minus her yellow raincoat emerges from behind a parked car. She's been hiding there for hours, nearly frozen. But too scared to move in case the sandwichman is lurking. Upstairs in an empty room her mother's crying. Unaware her daughter is so close. The positive note is, soon they'll be together. In the street, the snowploughs are cleaning up their first load of winter snow. And on the radio they have the press clips for early birds. What Ronald Reagan has for lunch. What scientists say about the fatal levels of chemicals in the food chain. And for gays, a warning about a new disease more fatal than any environmental poisoning. All treated in the witty language of a joke.

The heroine raises her head from the arborite table. Half awake, she sees a dreamface still looking through her window. Strangely familiar. Vines around its neck. Glistening as though it has risen from the sea. But outside (actually at the bottom of

The Main) only a large brown river runs. On the table lay the blue pages where she has copied passages from her diary. Open at the entry: *When I woke up the Papa Moon you gave me was floating on the water.*

The window fades to dawn. The heroine stands up. Drawing her blanket close, she takes the blue sheets and puts them on a violin stand beside the television. She steps back. Now they're at a distance. She smiles, liking how those pages on which she's written pain in curved letters change the context of the room. Making Janis' *It's all the same goddamned day* so clear. She looks around at last night's storm flashing on the television screen. At her own veined, slightly swollen feet standing on the old linoleum. Elements for a novel. But first she needs to eat. In the cupboard there's a hole where the tile's off. It's a wonder a rat hasn't come through. Never mind. She's not about to become one of those former revolutionaries hanging around health food stores, stocking up on engevita, ginseng, calcium, rice, fibre and verbena. Then finally moving into condominiums. Not yet anyway. She's got other things to do.

She searches for winter boots, finding only sneakers. Over the faded olive jumpsuit (it's a bit silly to dress so badly) she puts on the old fur jacket. Then steps out onto the front steps covered with green turf rug and a layer of snow. The rooftops are growing ever clearer in the grey dawn. High up, in an arc, a snowblower blows its charge. She walks forward on the white sidewalk (still faintly in the shadow of the night), then stops. Under the glass balcony that grey woman is waiting for Patchwork Rosanna. Mornings she always does that, waits under the balcony until Rosanna comes out and looks. Then big Rosanna in her patchwork robe, goes back in and puts the kettle on to make them tea. A door swings open into Rosanna's dark courtyard. The grey woman steps in mumbling something like: *... typical bailiff.* The heroine stands behind trying to listen. (She's never heard her talk.) *'The money,' said he,* mutters the grey woman, *'or I'm taking your Christmas tree.' The dirty muggins* (she's talking rapidly in a low excited voice). *They were taking off the lights the turkey came out of the oven the*

*children were hiding under the table he put his beefchopper on
my button breast. He said: 'Madame the rich get rich and the
poor get poorer.'* Then the grey woman throws her long grey
tangled hair back and sings a little ditty: *To Schwartz's Smoky
Meat / And to all the ragshop policemen on the street /
Montréal International Sheets / Lyrical Linen At Prices Most
Discrete / Lolly lolly jolly jolly / I know you love me / Because
I'm a stuffed hen in taxidermist's shop - - -* Seeing the heroine
she stops short.

The heroine keeps walking. Wondering why a woman can't
get what she wants without going into business on every front.
Social, political, economic, domestic. Each requiring a different
way of walking, a different way of talking. She looks instinctively for her own reflection in a store window. But it's as yet
too dark to see clearly. What if Marie is in Bagels'? Film crews
often breakfast there after working late. Looking tired,
rumpled, yet chic in their designer jeans and jackets. She grins
provocatively at her own tackiness. Marie a horreur du cheap.
Once the heroine said to her: 'Don't you ever watch a soap
opera, turn on popular music, read the comics or the horoscope?
I mean even in the interest of sociological research?' And Marie
answered: 'Je n'en ai pas besoin. J'ai grandi avec le quétaine.'

Her damp sneakers continue up The Main. Moving beside
her in the grey early winter light: the snowblower. And a kid
coming from a pharmacy carrying a sketchbook. His pale blue
eyes trained on the sky, gullsearching. But it's not 6 AM so the
light is still quite dim. He's headed towards the park where in
the summers of the 80s, the 70s men stroll with ever younger
brides. Where I saw you (my love) at the end of our reconciliation, pouring adoration over the girl with the green eyes. The
birds were singing wildly. Which really shocked me, for I
thought you'd left me to be with Venus. In a way I felt you'd
lied.

The heroine crosses northward at Rachel St. A block behind
her the grey woman is sitting down on a cement block drinking
Rosanna's tea. She keeps walking. Suddenly, up a staircase to
her left, a mother screams for joy as her freezing little daughter

falls against the door. The heroine takes it all in, her face a divided map of the present moment. One side savouring the sweetness of existence: the waking street, the kid's blue eyes gullsearching in the sky, Rosanna's tea. The other smarting against something vaguer. Something like what lies behind that song, popular in periods of unemployment, blasting forth as she opens the door of Bagels':

> if you're blue
> and you don't know wheere to go
> why don't you
> go where fashion sits
> puttin' on the Ritz
> puttin' on the Ritz

Eating, she thinks that in the 80s a story must be all smooth and shiny. For this pretends to be the decade of appearances. Like a photo of the silhouettes of figures passing on the street outside the restaurant window. Or the beautiful faces of those women (Marie's colleagues?), lit by a small light at one of the diner's tables. She actually loves the ambiance of the period.

But walking back down The Main, just past the staircase where the mother hugged her lost girl, she thinks: Yet I feel this terrible violence in me. In any story, it will break the smoothness of the surface.

Looking up she notices she's standing in the shadow of a building that broke the zoning laws when constructed, because so high. Leaving the surrounding smaller houses eternally in deep shade day and night. Once she even plotted with another woman friend to blow the building up. It was only a joke between them. But she and her friend talked and talked about how to do it. Obsessively at restaurant tables over cups of coffee. Each one knowing the other wasn't serious. Each one also knowing they needed something to salve their incredible frustrations with the left as well, they said, as with patriarchal society. (Her friend is married to a doctor.)

Now, standing there in the shadow of the cold wall of grey, with gulls circling overhead and the mother's joyous scream still threaded through her mind, the heroine feels that old desire for a terrible explosion.

She thinks: Maybe I should talk to someone.

Startled by a sudden glimpse of her reflection in a window, she thinks: Maybe I should get a job. Then I could buy one of those second-hand men's coats trendy women wear this year. I could probably get one cheap. Or else one of those beautiful expresso pots I saw in the window up the street.

She walks a little farther, wondering.

She passes the grey woman sitting in her long skirt on the cement block.

She thinks: Maybe I should talk to her.

She thinks: The question is, is it possible to create Paradise in this Strangeness?

In the grey light, she's standing on the sidewalk (snowy of course), her pale red curls her one sign of beauty. Looking to the left, the right.

She –

SHEILA GREENBERG

Gail Scott was born in Ottawa and grew up in a bilingual community in Eastern Ontario. She worked as a journalist for several years, writing about Québec culture and politics for *The Gazette*, as well as contributing to the *Globe and Mail* and *Maclean's*. Her first book, *Spare Parts*, was published by Coach House Press in March, 1982. Her fiction and criticism have appeared in several periodicals including *Room of One's Own*, *Writing*, *The Canadian Forum*, *La Nouvelle Barre du Jour*, *Nuit Blanche*, and *Spirale*, a French-language critical review of which she was a founding editor. She is co-editor of *Tessera*, a bilingual journal of contemporary women's writing.

The critics on *Spare Parts*, Gail Scott's first book with Coach House (a collection of five stories that trace a woman's development from puberty to maturity during the turbulent 60s):

It is intellectually satisfying in a way that much feminist realism is not. It is a hard place Gail Scott finds herself, but it is rich, too, in the complexities of sexuality, language and culture. She confronts, attacks, and transcends her own failure in making what Phyllis Webb has called 'a structure for our loss.'
JANE RULE

Gail Scott's writing is vivid and keen: details stand isolated in a light that is unnaturally bright and unusually harsh. The rhythms of the prose are strong, almost incantatory.... It is good. It is powerful. That is all that matters.
MAGGIE HELWIG

Reading *Spare Parts* [is] a very intense experience. It is not a book that romanticizes nostalgia. It lives up to its title by paring recollection to its essence and providing us with only what is left over, the parts that remain when the pieces have been put back together. It is essential reading for a generation whose life never quite matched the ideals that were promised to it.
BRIAN CHARLTON

The whole work is as densely textured as a poem, with extraordinarily rich symbolic imagery, and it is this aspect that gives the book its emotional power.... Woman and her experiences as a collection of spare parts. It's a powerful image and a stylistic mode which Gail Scott crafts with great care in this surprisingly poignant and often funny book.
CHRISTINE ST. PETER